Blender's Story

BLENDER'S STORY

Book 1 of the

Servants of the Wheel Series

BETH SCHLUTER

CONTENTS

This book is dedicated to all lovers of Fantasy.
. Those who dream of different worlds filled with magic and romance.
Thank you to my past publishers, William & Brown,
who believed in me and allowed me to dream.
Thank you to Amazon for enabling my Fantasy novels to live on.

Chapter 1

My heart yearns for something. I'm not sure what. To be
liked? No. To be talented? No. To be a part of something
great? No, I already am. What then do I yearn for? To be
respected? - Perhaps. To be taken seriously? Definitely.
Meanwhile, I try to keep out of everybody's way as much
as possible. I have a talent for that at least.

They all pass me by unseen, engrossed in their stories,
some true, some not. From all my blending, I know who
to trust and who isn't worth the effort. If they could see I
was there, their conversation would turn to me, or maybe
not. Some wouldn't care if I heard their true opinion.

The stone wall smells musty. Does anyone ever clean it?
The dust is in my hair and fingers and I almost sneeze,
but I mustn't. That would give me away. They've nearly

all passed me now, so I can get out. Good, one quick glance and the passageway is clear. I detach myself from the wall's grip and walk on towards the Wheel Room like the others, to find out what this emergency is we've been summoned for.

I hardly ever get chosen though. Well, why would they bother? Axl nearly always chooses Brava for her bravery and courage or Stretch for his adaptability and initiative. Of course, they would. They look the part, tall, strong, and well respected- unlike me. Skinny and small I'm hardly noticeable. And they always choose wisely, to ensure success in their missions.

I wonder what it is today. A lost Past, or a poisoned village maybe...? Perhaps the world's falling apart? Ha! Then they certainly won't need me, I'm just part of the background, there to make up the numbers.

"Hey Mouse! You skulking in dark corners again?" Shadow's booming voice fills the corridor behind me. Damn, I thought he'd already gone ahead. Why did I have to be caught up by him, of all people? I turn around briefly to respond, trying to keep a cool head.

"Isn't that what you do? Or are you just late getting out of bed again? Nothing new there."

His smug grin catches up with me, his dark hair dishevelled as usual. I took a deep breath. "Don't you ever comb your hair? You look like Pinni's stuffed dog, except he's got more appeal," I said. He laughs but nudges me hard until I crash into the wall.

"At least I've got a life. Not like you, too scared to do anything- Mouse." He spat the word out, like it was something dirty. " Try not to fall asleep at the Wheel today!"

His gangly form struts away in front of me and I smile at his stupid jacket logo. "Hate You" about sums him up.

The dark, oaken doors to the Wheel Room are wide open, ready to invite us in and the candlelight from within dances upon the dim passage outside. Lots of loud voices come from the room, so all of them are there then, waiting for Axl and Pinni- and me. I'm usually last, so I take a deep breath and walk in, but find I am not the only Servant missing in the circle.

"Aw, look who it isn't!" Grinder shouts out, as soon as he sees me, his leather booted feet resting on the edge of the Wheel table. He wouldn't dare do that if Axl were here- or Pinni, come to that. None of the others laugh with him and Shadow jeers as he throws a ball of parchment at me. I duck and he misses, hitting the door instead.   I hurry to find my seat in the circle.

I sit between Stretch and Pax, who are both all right. They are both friendly, except when Stretch is having an off day. Then he can be a bit contrary. I have never heard them say bad things about me. Shadow, unfortunately, sits to Pax's right and has a habit of lobbing bits into my hair when Axl or Pinni aren't looking. He's a real pain in the rectum.

"You okay Blender?" Pax asks cheerily. "Yeah, fine thanks. Do you know what the emergency is?"

7

He leans closer to whisper, he usually hears things on the grapevine from Patience, her being pally with one of Axl's inner circle of friends. But often, he's unwilling to betray her trust and mostly says little of what he knows.

" I heard it's something serious, about... Oh, here they come." He stands up straight, as does everyone else, for Axl and Pinni arrive to start the meeting. The empty chair in the Wheel captures my attention- Brava's not here.

Axl glides in, her glistening ebony skin magnificent in her scarlet and silver cloak, looking the part, regal and imposing, the sign of authority. Even the pain in the butts respect her and listen to what she says, and they generally listen to nobody else except Pinni. Axl makes an excellent Wheel Governor; she is wise and what she says goes. Although she always looks kindly upon me, I can't help but feel like I shouldn't be here, being so unlike the others. Shadow once called me the runt of the litter and I feel he's not far wrong. He and Grinder take pleasure in generally making my life a misery.

Candles flutter on the sconces as the Governor and her Deputy pass by the edges of the Wheel, flames magnifying with the movement of air, as though some excess energy passes on from their bodies to the sconces. The room is silent as Axl and Pinni make their way towards the centre, faces sombre. Pinni's eyes flick over to Brava's empty seat briefly. His face shows his distaste as this long thin nose looks down upon his narrow chin.

Pinni goes to stand near the centre of the Wheel, which is our cue to bow our heads to welcome our leader, Axl, as she takes the centre hub, to commence proceedings. Axl always sits in the central position, with Pinni by her side, both facing opposite directions, so their eyes theoretically, maintain a view of all of us Servants of the Wheel.

Pinni looks so drab compared to Axl. Although tall like her, his weathered face is stern looking and his grey features are not helped by his sombre black and grey robes, which always look like they belong in a museum. They look ancient and moth-eaten, but then again, so does he, he is ancient. Both are. They have controlled The Wheel together for over four hundred years, although Axl only looks to be in her fifties to any Normals.

At the end of the twelve wedges of the Wheel sit the twelve Servants of the Wheel, of which I am one- believe it or not. Together, we create and maintain a balance in the World. As Servants, we are tasked with fixing any problems, big or small, that occur in Gardia and the outer World, to avoid Chaos getting a foothold. Sometimes Axl or Pinni selects Servants for a task, and sometimes Servants themselves volunteer. I have never been on an important task as yet, nor felt the inclination to put myself forward. I know only too well what the other Servants' responses would be.

 Axl doesn't seem to notice Brava's empty chair, barely glancing in that direction. But Pinni's steely stare shoots another glance towards it and he sniffs as he lowers himself to his seat. We all sit down and await Axl's instructions.

9

How embarrassing for Brava if she comes in now-nobody turns up late at the Wheel. Never- Totally unheard of. And she, the favourite of both Axl and the Servants too. Her bravery, strength and heroism are renowned throughout all Gardia and her courage as a Servant is unsurpassable. Whatever the reason for her being late, it is just not done.

Eyes flit nervously towards the door and back towards Brava's seat, wondering what will happen when she finally appears. Will the Kingpin of the Wheel get a talking to in front of us all? We all hold our breath in anticipation as we hear footsteps approaching. But it is not Brava.

Pinni accepts the roll of parchment from his aide and hands it to Axl after quickly scanning it, with a slight inclination of the head. His face is even more grave than usual. As the centre hub begins to slowly rotate, Axl reads in silence then places the parchment on her table. Now she looks across at us all, her eyes for once pensive, with a hint of moisture glinting in the candlelight. Something bad has taken place, that much is obvious, and I straighten up in my chair to await the details.

She seems to be composing herself to speak and I note a slight tremble in her hand and now I am nervous too. Axl is never nervous; she is the calmest of us all. She clears her throat and finally speaks in a quiet but sombre tone.

"Servants of the Wheel, I'm afraid I bring you ill tidings. This morning I was woken by the sound of Wheel Screech, brief, but clear..."

A shiver ran through my spine. Wheel Screech can only be heard by the Governor, when someone is in mortal danger somewhere. She continued, with a glance towards Brava's seat. "This parchment confirms it. Brava cannot be found anywhere in Gardia. She is missing and in mortal danger."

A gasp rippled through the Servants as we took in the implication. Hope's gentle voice was heard saying "Surely not missing? Might she not simply have been delayed on a mission by herself? Perhaps so urgent she did not have time to approach you about it?"

Axl attempted a small smile at Hope's belief. "I wish it were so, but I will have it confirmed, one way or another." Axl looked directly at me, and I swallowed hard. "Blender, perhaps you can see if she has taken anything from the Wall of Keys for us?" She smiled encouragingly.

All eyes stared at me now. Axl had never asked anything of me before and I'm sure they wondered why she would ask this of me. I nodded and closed my eyes, blotting out Shadow's scowl.

I focused my thoughts on the dark cavern where the Wall of Keys was carved into the stone walls. Here, the keys to different elements in the world lay, attached to the wall, each a different glowing color to indicate its use. As Servants, we all were taught their meaning and how to invoke their power when undertaking a quest. I could now see it clearly before me, the brightly glowing colors lighting up the dim cavern. I checked each niche carefully to see if any keys were missing. I opened my eyes again, to find everyone's faces staring at me, most in confusion, some in anticipation.

"None of the ten keys are missing Governor Axl. They are all still in their niches." She nodded sombrely. "Thank you, Blender. It is as I feared then, Brava has been taken."

Eyes now turned from me to Axl, some still filled with incredulity at my apparent ability to see things. "Taken? Who could possibly overwhelm Brava? She's so ... strong and .... clever." Grace said, her perfect face full of puzzlement.

"That's exactly what worries me," Axl replied. " Whoever or whatever has taken her, must be very powerful and extremely clever to have infiltrated Gardia like this. Our security is breached. We must all be vigilant while I send out some of you Servants to try and retrieve her."

The unease mounted in the room, as Axl's eyes took us all in. Brava was the best of us. Nobody could match her strength and courage, so whoever was to undertake the task of retrieval would face extreme danger. Perhaps dark powers. For it could only be the Servants of Chaos that could have achieved such a feat. For once, there was a distinct lack of volunteers, and I did not blame them. To take on the dark ones is to face death. Axl's eyes returned to me, and I froze.

"Blender, I think this is a task that would suit you best. I believe you alone have the right powers to find our Servant and bring her back to us. Whatever is holding her is obviously a grave threat, so I will ask you to choose two Servants to help you in your quest. Choose wisely."

My heart fell into my stomach. Was I really hearing this? She's choosing me? I scanned the faces around the Wheel and found them all staring at me, as sceptical as I was, but there was something more in some of their faces this time. It was a new respect. Axl had faith in me, and I was not about to let her down. I swallowed hard and found my voice.

"You do me a great honour Governor Axl. I will undertake this quest willingly and find this danger that dared infiltrate Gardia. And I pledge to do all I can to eliminate it or die trying."

Axl smiled and nodded slowly, her hands no longer trembling, but knitted together before her on the table.

"Thank you, Blender, I expected no less. And who will you choose to accompany you on this quest?" I looked again at the faces, some eager, some scared, some startled and I slowly replied, "I choose Arch.... and Patience." A collective sigh rang out from either relief or regret for not being chosen. The two smiled at me, for which I was thankful. Pax squeezed my hand under the table in encouragement as he too smiled. He whispered, "A good choice, well done." I nodded and smiled in return.

Axl stood and we all did the same. Pinni made a brief statement. "Those not in the quest come with me. We will begin improving the security around Gardia. Those chosen, stay." The Servants led out after him, leaving just Axl and us three chosen behind at the Wheel.

13

Axl's staff shone, brightening up the dripping tunnels as we made our way to the Cavern of Keys. I thought hard about which keys to take with me on this quest. I need to cover as many bases as I can within my limit of three keys. I hoped I'd pick well.

As we walked along, Arch thanked me for choosing him and vowed to help in any way he could to find Brava and bring her home. His attitude has changed slightly since the revelation that I was a Visionary. He's always been quite civil towards me, but now, there is a new respect in his eyes. Patience is already a good friend. She always talks to me around Gardia and we hang out with Stretch and Pax in our free time. None of them have ever asked what my abilities are. It didn't matter to them; they just accepted me as I am.

I felt a bit guilty about not choosing my friends Stretch or Pax, but I think I chose wisely for the task. Although Patience and Arch are not particularly great fighters, their supportive skills should ensure smooth running on our quest together. I guess we must use the best of our skills somehow to get us to where we want to be.

"Here we are." Axl led inside, where denser sounds of dripping water echoed somewhere in the distance. A musty, earthy smell filled the stale air within as we walked towards the platform that held the glowing keys in the center of the huge cave.

The large rocky stone before us held upon it an ancient carved rectangle, a bit like a giant doorway, surrounded by intricate carvings of all the elements. Embedded in the rectangle, inside various shaped niches, were the glowing keys. They were placed at random intervals, and none shone more brightly than any other. Each looked different to the others. Only a Servant on a quest could extract the keys. They were held in position by some ancient magic.

Axl stood aside as I stepped forward to gaze at the odd shapes. Not really key shapes in the conventional sense at all. Some were prisms, others mere slivers, or marbles of unknown fabrication. Their bright colors reflected on all our faces, giving us a magical glow of our own.

"I know you will choose wisely Blender." Axl smiled as she inclined her head. I felt privileged to have her speak directly to me. My mind raced, trying to recall the purpose of each color, as I stood before this great Wall of Keys. My teachings came back to me instantly and I was relieved. I breathed deeply.

"I take the Viridian, for the Earth," I said. Arch nodded approvingly. "And I choose the Ultramarine for the Oceans." "Good choice." whispered Patience.

I looked at the remaining options and was debating whether to take the key to Fire or the Wind. I hesitated before finally making my choice. "And I also take the Ivory for the Spirit World." All three eyed me sharply at this final choice. Axl's eyes were questioning, but she said nothing. It was Patience who spoke.

"Are you sure Blender? That's... A very bold choice." I eyed them all nervously, but my heart was steadfast. "Yes,

15

I'm sure. I have a good feeling about it, I take Earth, Oceans and the Spirit World."

Axl indicated for me to step forward to collect my keys as my co-Servants stepped aside. I held my hand out before me and performed the incantation for extraction in one of the Ancient Languages:

"R'wyn dewis agoriad y Mor, y Ddeuar a Chartref yr Ysbrydion, y tri i fy helpu i ddarganfod ac adennill Brava, ein Morwyn o ble bynnag y bydd hi. Ar rhan Gardia mi wnaf eu defnyddio yn ofalus."

One by one, the three keys detached themselves from their niches and floated into my hand, their warmth filling me with hope, and I clenched my fingers tightly around them as they shrank in size to dissolve into my palm. Axl smiled and nodded her approval.

"Now we will go into the Cave of Artefacts to choose your aids for your quest." She led along the cavern closer towards the sound of tumbling water in the distance.

This would be the first time for me to be there, as I had not been chosen for a proper quest before. Both Patience and Arch had been chosen by others previously, so they knew what to expect. I only knew from my readings what should lie there. I began to feel nervous again.

We walked along the slippery, narrow path that lay behind a wide waterfall, its graphite waters pooling into froth some fifty meters below. The spray drenched us, but Axl seemed to have a film of air around her through which no water permeated. It was intriguing.

Beyond the waterfall lay the Cave of Artefacts. It was like some pirate's treasure trove, where several gleaming gold and jewelled items were strewn along the walls, clefts and floor space. Interspersed were ancient looking tools, the like of which I'd never seen before. Many artefacts lay on altars of stone, some so small they fitted in your hand. Others large enough to stand alone, each with a special power of its own.

I stared, open-mouthed, as I stood looking down upon them from the ledge upon which the path descended. Each of these, I had been taught, held special abilities to aid a Servant in their quest. To see their images in books did not do them justice, for these were truly magnificent to behold in the flesh. Some exuded such power as to make your skin tingle as you neared them.

"How am I going to choose from all these fantastic artefacts?" I thought to myself. *"What if I choose wrongly? It could ruin my chances of retrieving Brava..."*

"You choose first Patience," I said. "You've done this before. I trust your choice." She smiled and nodded and walked purposefully towards a dark red bow and quiver resting against a heavy chest. "I choose the Bow of Hearts for my first object."

"What would you choose first Arch?" I asked. His eyes searched and then he found it. "I choose the Sword of Glass for my first artefact," he said. "A good choice for otherworldly creatures," Axl commented. "And your first choice Blender?"

I headed towards a plain black sword in its runed leather sheath upon the wall. "I choose the Sword of Justice first," I said. All three nodded their approval.

"Good choices so far." Axl said. "Now for your second choices?"

The three of us headed towards our chosen items and held them up.

"The Orb of Light." Patience said.

"The Shield of Darkness." Arch said.

"And I choose the Stone of Power."

"All good choices." Axl nodded. "Now make your choices carefully for your final artifacts" The three of us searched through the cave for the items we wanted. Mine was hard to find as it was so small. "I will take Elinor's Tears." Arch held up a black vial. "The Horn of Plenty" Patience said with a grin. "We certainly won't starve on our quest." Axl and Arch smiled too. Finally, I found the tiny white shell, nestling upon a jeweled gauntlet on the table."And I choose the Shell of Echoes for my final artefact."

Axl eyed us all sombrely, the glow of her staff glittering upon the jewelled and mirrored items surrounding us. Their reflections danced upon the cave, like a kaleidoscope of colour in the otherwise dim and dank cave.

Axl spoke softly, but in her eyes, I saw a glint of fear. I felt there was something she wasn't telling us, but it wasn't my place to ask.

" I chose well, as did you Blender. I see why all of you have made your choices and I pray that you will use them wisely on your quest. Brava's life lies in your hands," she hesitated then added, "as perhaps, does all of Gardia."

Gardia itself, I had not factored into my thoughts. But of course, if Brava, the strongest and most able of us all had been taken from here, then it was vital that we found the infiltrators and destroyed them too. None of us could afford to allow such a breach to continue.

"I will accompany you to the Drift, after that, you are on your own. Come, follow me." Axl guided us through the twisting and narrow path towards our fate.

Chapter 2

We arrived at the Drift- portal to the worlds, at the end of a short twisting tunnel beyond the Cave of Artefacts. It hummed of power before us, its wispy silvery threads of mist writhing within the shape of the gateway. It was hypnotizing to watch if you stood there too long, so I ventured forth and steeled myself.

One by one we entered the glistening mist. Axl's final words of encouragement echoed in my ears, as we travelled through into the Outer Worlds. Mists of scenes flitted by our eyes as we floated on through the Corridor of Sighs.

Sounds of many Worlds rang in our ears, beckoning us towards them. The creaking of boughs as the wind passes through them in the forest realms. The rush of waves upon the ocean shores, crashing onto hidden rocks and cliffs. The screech of giant birds as they fly, hovering on streams of warm air as they search for prey. The gritty shifting of sands as they move continually in the deserts and so many more sounds sought us out. It was my quest, my decision which to choose and the weight of all those Worlds weighed down heavily upon me as I closed my eyes to focus my mind.

Arch and Patience waited quietly for my guidance. I knew Patience's talents included hearing things none of us others could, but she rightly left me to decide my options. They floated in the corridor with me, awaiting my sign, to show where I would go first. My mind hovered over the different scenarios, but nothing in particular drew me forth at first, then a vision of a forest glade with a cart in it sprang into my head. I must do this instinctively then. I opened my eyes and pointed my sword towards the forested lands to the East and the two clung onto me as I was swept on the wispy tide ever downwards to the Outer World below.

My body felt weightless as we were free-falling down to the lands below. The breeze whipped my hair across my eyes several times and I'm sure Patience was glad she'd tied back her red hair that day. Arch was sensible, keeping his hair short, so the wind did not bother him at all. He grinned at me as I battled with my hair. Why didn't I tie it back today of all days?

We cascaded down onto the edge of one of Gardia's ancient forests, the GrunWald, where a storm brewed in the skies above. The trees next to us threw their branches low in the ever-increasing wind, almost toppling Patience as she landed. Their veined boughs creaked in protest.

"Wow! Couldn't you have picked a better day?" Patience ran for shelter under a huge, gnarled, old oak, as twigs and debris flew around us in the gale. Arch and I ran to join her, narrowly avoiding being struck by a large branch, which had just been torn from an Elm nearby. Maybe I should have chosen Causia, she could have got rid of the storm for us.

"Sorry, it must have come on suddenly, as we descended," I said. "It just looked a bit breezy when I looked down. We'd better go further inside the forest, where we'll get more shelter." I led the way deeper in as Arch and Patience protected themselves from further damage by using Arch's Shield of Darkness, which enlarges to the size required when invoked.

I soon found us a quieter area, sheltered from the worst of the storm under the widespread canopy of the forest's ancient oaks. Although much darker here, at least we were safer from flying debris.

"We got here just in time- it's starting to rain very heavily," Patience said. Even though the canopy prevented us from seeing the sky and witnessing it, Patience's hearing was exemplary, and I hoped to make use of it frequently to help us in our quest. Peering from under his shield at the dense canopy above, Arch now hooked the Shield back on his shoulder. When it wasn't needed it reduced in size.

"Can you hear anything else Patience?" I asked.

She closed her eyes in concentration, turning slowly for a minute or two to face different directions, before opening her eyes again.

"Only the normal sounds you'd expect from a forest, although I did think for a moment that I heard a voice. It wasn't Brava's though. Probably someone collecting mushrooms." "Near or far?" Arch asked.

"Far inside the centre of the forest- in that direction." Patience pointed. With the dense canopy saving us from being drenched or wind-swept, we made our way through the thick forest in search of signs of a path. We used the Orb to light our way as the canopy thickened, blocking out the sky above us. We talked quietly as we walked, listening, and keeping a lookout for traces of movement. I found it curious that I saw no animals in this part of the forest.

"What made you choose the forest?" Patience asked as she held a notched arrow in preparation for any trouble. She could sense the strangeness in the air too.

"I think I chose it mainly because it is the area closest to the Drift's invocation. It just made sense. Anyone who came to Gardia would have likely passed through here to get to us. Plus, I had a brief flicker of an image set in a forest to check out."

"Did you see Brava in this image?" asked Arch. I shook my head and told him what I saw.

"But surely the cart would be long gone from here by now," he said.

"More than likely, but... I can pick up signs of their passing- see where they are headed. I've just got to find a good starting point first. - A path maybe?" Arch nodded, but I doubt he fully understood.

Dead elms allowed gaps to form in the canopy from time to time and on our way to the centre the wind was so strong that we could barely walk upright, even in the sheltered woodland.

"We need to tie ourselves to some trees until this passes," I said. "Otherwise, we'll be sucked into the skies. I'm sure I feel a tornado coming this way."

Patience had the presence of mind to ask the Horn of Plenty for ropes to bind us. I'd forgotten its ability to provide things other than food and drink and was now thankful for her choice.

"But there have never been any tornados in this woodland realm before." Arch said. "Why have things changed over here?"

"I have a distinct impression that it's got something to do with our presence here and those who took Brava," I said, as I tied myself securely to a tree.

The tornado hit minutes after we secured ourselves and our gear. Branches and leaves flew past our faces with such force I thought even a simple leaf could slice open my face at the speed it travelled. The force of the wind lifted us off our feet and only the ropes kept us from being sucked to our deaths into the skies. The sounds of the thunderous winds hurt my ears and I tried to protect them with my hands, but the force of it prevented me from using my arms effectively. They were just sucked upwards by the whirling winds.

We looked at each other worriedly as some trees were uprooted and sent hurtling into the darkening skies beyond. Our voices could not be heard above the noise, so we did not speak. All we could do was watch as branches and leaves were sucked upwards into the dark abyss by the whirling wind, never to be seen again.

This is no ordinary tornado. It should have moved on by now... It's staying in position above us. The thoughts swam in my mind. We were being targeted by something unknown and I had to do something, but what?

I used all my strength to force my hand forward. Every second was a battle between my muscles and the force of the wind. But after three agonising minutes of willpower, I did it. My hand activated the stone. I clasped it tight in my fist. It began to warm up instantly.

I closed my eyes and concentrated on the invocation of power...

"Dwy'n gofyn am nerth Y Garreg I gael gwared ar y storm sydd yn cadw ni'n garcharwyr. Yn enw Gardia, am byth."

A glow emanated from my pocket and burst forth in a blinding light that tore through the woodland canopy above. It sent shards of light into the dark morass above us, and I felt the winds immediately begin to abate around me. Seconds later the three of us dropped to the ground once more, tethered to our trees, but no longer impotent to move normally. The sounds of the storm withered and

25

died and soon there was nothing but the flutter of a warm breeze dancing through the canopy above. The storm and its tornado were gone.

"What did you do?" Arch asked, relieved. He untied his rope like the rest of us, glad to be safe once more.

"I invoked the strength of the Stone of Power. This time to dissipate the storm, rather than create one. I wasn't sure if it would do that, but I'm glad it did. I was lucky. And luckier still- as the storm raised me up, I saw a valuable sign."

"Well done," said Patience. "It was an un-natural storm, wasn't it?"

"Yes. Whoever sent it, probably took Brava. They know we're looking for her. We must be on our guard, at all times."

Arch wound the ropes into a loop and tied them to his pack. "You said you'd spotted some sign. What did you see?" I walked over towards the gnarled bark of an ancient tree ten paces away and crouched beside it.

"See here? The bark has a new scar upon it, a foot from its base and the ground beside it has a deep rut. A cart or something has created that, rubbing past it. I will find out what or who did it before we continue on our way."

"What the?" Arch's mouth was wide open, jaw dropped in surprise, as I disappeared into the bark of the ancient tree. My body melded itself into every pore of the bark, until there was nothing to be seen of me. I was completely blended.

"How the heck did he do that?" Patience was wide-eyed too, staring as my body disappeared. I could not answer her until I had done the recall.

A slight breeze ruffled the leaves around me, then a rabbit bounced out of nowhere. It stopped and sniffed the air and dug in the leaf mold for a moment before moving on again. Small creatures moved in the undergrowth nearby, heard but unseen. Day rapidly turned to night, and I could hear an owl's cry, somewhere in the distance. A mouse scurried quickly across the leaves, out of sight, then it was quiet for a long time.

As I became aware of a new moon, I heard voices. The bark tingled in my skin as I prepared myself for what was to come. The sound of creaking cartwheels and horses approached. Yes, I smell the horses, their sweat and manure filling my senses.

My skin went rigid as I sensed her presence. Brava! I watched in horror as the party of dark creatures passed with their quarry, cackling and jesting about their conquest. I felt a scratch on my skin, as a cartwheel skimmed the bark. Several more strange, dark horses followed, transporting several foul creatures and I held my breath trying not to smell their rancid stench. Then they were gone.

I had counted two moons. I pulled myself away from the bark and reformed before Patience and Arch. They stared, mouths agape, trying to comprehend what they'd seen. I straightened up, stretching my limbs to ease them back into reality. I checked my ankle where I'd felt the cartwheel scratch, but nothing was there now.

"Blender..." Patience stated simply, returning to her senses. "It's what you do- you blend into things?" I nodded.

"Yes."

"Why? Why did you do that?" Arch asked quietly, finally finding his voice. He hadn't moved a muscle the whole time I'd been in the Past. I dusted myself off, pulling moss out of my hair and replied. "It's how I see what has passed before. I became the tree and saw what it witnessed."

They did not understand. I couldn't blame them. They both had their own unique qualities; this was one of mine.

"I saw the creatures who took Brava. They passed by this way two nights ago. She was on a cart, inside a black coffin, pulled by other worldly horses. They were all on horseback. Foul creatures. I would guess they were from the Lands of Chaos by the look of them."

Their faces fell, knowing the horror that we would now all face.

"Was she... Alive?" asked Patience. I shook my head grimly. "I couldn't tell. She was entombed in this huge black coffin. I did not see her, but I felt her presence. By the size of the coffin, it had to be her inside."

Their faces said it all. I would not blame them if they'd wanted to turn back, but I knew they wouldn't. It is why I chose them.

"Let's go. They've got a good head start on us."

We were exhausted as we ran, trying to gain ground on our friend. It was easier to follow their tracks now that we knew what to look for. The wheel imprints were evident in areas of soft ground, but strangely, we saw no sign of any horses' hooves. Perhaps they were shaded.

The forest kept its canopy over us for a day and night and we finally found ourselves lacking in strength to go on. Patience dropped to the ground, panting.

"It's no good, my legs are like lead weights. I haven't the strength to carry on running, I'm sorry."

"It's all right. We all need to rest and eat, to gather our strength. We'll wait here a while. We've surely gained much ground upon them, and I would think they will need a rest too." I sat opposite her, my back to a tree to lean on.

Patience unhooked the Horn of Plenty from her pack and drew forth some food and drink for us all. We sat together as the darkness drew in around us and we made a small fire to keep us warm.

"I never knew I could run so far without stopping." Arch said between sips of wine. "I suppose none of us know what we are capable of until we really try."

"I think you're right. I don't know about you two, but I'm so tired I can hardly keep my eyes open. Shall we take it in turns to take watch?" "No need," Arch said. " The Shield of Darkness will protect us. I will invoke its power until we are fully rested. Nobody will find us under its cover."

Of course. I'd forgotten in my tired state. The Shield protects all beneath it, as it creates a patch of darkness that hides whatever is in its shadow. Even with our firelight, we will not be seen under its protection.

I lay my head down wearily onto my pack and fell asleep instantly. My body relaxed into a deep sleep and for a long while I simply slept, bone weary. In time, I began to have visions. Glimpses of reality, perhaps? They were cryptic and unsettling.

The night around us was filled with movement. Rustling of creatures scuttling through the undergrowth, some animals foraging whilst others made their night sounds to ward off intruders. Gentle breezes threw leaves and twigs near our faces, making our sleep sporadic. In the end, we got used to all of it and slept like the dead.

"Wake up Blender." I felt a hand grasp my arm, gently stirring me out of my sleep. I opened my eyes to find Patience's blue eyes looking down at me, her long red hair trailing across my chest. It was morning.

"What's happened? Is something wrong?" I asked, rubbing my eyes. Arch's deep voice replied behind me. "You were dreaming, calling out things... Garbled stuff."

I sat up, trying to recall what I had seen, whilst Patience plaited her hair, then I began to see the pieces that unsettled me. "Oh. I hope they were just nightmares and not reality."

"What? What did you see?" Arch asked, standing above me, and handing me a drink.

"I saw. Limbs. Dismembered limbs... I think they could be Brava's. They had dark skin like hers. Oh god no. Please don't let it be so." Patience's face crumpled with fear. "Surely it was merely a nightmare. Don't you think?"

I didn't know, but I reassured her with my answer. "Most likely. I do get them a lot when I'm very tired." "Come, let's eat and be on our way. Daylight is upon us." Arch helped me up.

We ate quickly and felt refreshed, ready for another grueling day's running. Arch had already deactivated his shield, so they must have let me lie in a bit. I accepted the proffered food gladly and swept away the night's visions, hoping it was not too late.

Chapter 3

Darkness was fast approaching when we stopped for rest again. Autumn days are short for searches. We had covered many miles of forest tracks, but still found ourselves to be no nearer to the cart. Many tracks were misleading, and I think they were deliberately set to delay us. It was a pity we did not have horses of our own. That was one thing the Horn of Plenty did not provide, unfortunately.

I gathered some sticks to form a fire. The nights could be particularly cold without one. There was plenty of kindling after the storm, scattered about the forest floor.

"This forest seems endless, but it has to end soon surely," I said, looking beyond the small clearing for signs of anything different. But all I saw were trees, tall, vast tree trunks with twisting limbs outstretched, entwining with each other to form a dense evergreen canopy. The Devil himself would have difficulty finding anyone in this. The low branches formed their own Shield of Darkness tonight.

The small clearing was no more than two hundred feet square, and a stout oaken branch twisted its way across it to provide cover for us. We sat around the fire, warming ourselves, as Patience drew out food from the Horn. We were so glad of her choice; it was a godsend in a place such as this. We had no time to hunt for food or gather berries.

We ate quietly, the sound of the crackling fire filling the silence. My mind returned to the previous night's dreams, and I thought of Brava entombed in that coffin, wondering if she had even been alive.

Suddenly Patience's head shot up, as did Arch's, both eyeing the same direction. My skin tingled, as I felt it too.

"Demons!"

I drew my sword the same time as Arch. Patience set her arrow ready on her bow, eyeing the dense treeline nervously. I had little time to react as a black-veiled creature descended upon me from above, sending me off balance, and tumbling to the ground. It was heavy and foul smelling, its long-nailed fingers dug into my skin as it tried to find purchase. My sword had dropped out of my hand somewhere and my eyes urgently searched for it.

I only realized as the creature flipped aside onto the ground beside me, that Patience had struck it in the heart with her arrow. It lay dissolving on the ground, taking its foul stench with it. I barely had time to thank her, as several other creatures fell upon us from all around. This time I held my sword tightly and swung its deadly blade through two demons rushing towards me. They fell upon impact with the Sword of Justice.

Arch scythed his way through a larger demon to my left, renting its body with deep gouges from his Sword of Glass. Although it could wound, I knew it could not kill on land. So, I raced to add my own sword's power into effect, and it fell to its death upon my sword's touch. It dropped like a stone, causing the ground to shake around us.

Patience's arrows struck three demons. One had pierced the heart of two demons simultaneously as they came running towards her, one behind the other. Another was struck in the tree line before it had even time to advance. They dissolved at the arrows' touch. Each time an arrow was used another took its place in the quiver.

We whirled around in search for more demons, and they came advancing upon us together, in a circle from the tree line, cackling and jeering, revealing their foul fangs and breathing out rancid air. Patience fired one arrow after another into them as Arch and I cut the rest through with our swords. My own sword cut the final threads of life from Arch's conquests as they fell, withering on the ground, until none were left standing.

"I think we got them all." Patience gasped as she returned the heart arrow in her hand, keeping her eyes ever vigilant for more demons in the trees. But none came.

"Yes, I think we did. Thank you both." I said, relieved I had chosen the Sword of Justice. It's very touch on the skin ensured success.

"You did your own part too. Without your sword, we might have perished." Arch said. "Let's hope that there are no more. I'd better put my Shield up, after all, to make sure we are left alone." "Good idea. It seems to be our best night defence so far."

"Were they the same demons you saw taking Brava?" Patience asked. She tidied her arrows back in the quiver.

"Similar," I said. "Now they know we're on their trail. I guess we'd better use the Shield to protect us each night. The question is, how did demons get beyond the Veil ?"

Morning arrived with a certain chill. Autumn was moving closer into Winter. The first wisps of snowflakes floated downwards with the falling leaves and started clinging to the ground. Soon the canopy would be thinner. Only the evergreens would prevail.

We drew our cloaks about us and headed on after breakfast, hoping for an end to this vast forest maze. After trekking for a few hours, I began to imagine things watching us, nervous of any more demons lurking, waiting to pounce from the shadowed trees. But none came. Instead, the forest ended abruptly.

We lost the trail in the snow, a mile or so back and now we stood looking down upon a vast ocean from atop a forested cliff. Gardia was completely landlocked, so where were we? The shore was thirty feet below us.

"Do you think they took a boat from here?" Patience asked. I peered into the distance, trying to find any signs of vessels on the horizon.

"If they did, they're long gone," I said. "I can't see any ships or boats anywhere ahead. Mind you, the low cloud cover doesn't help visibility. We need to get down to the shore so I can check it out."

I'm sure they wondered what my idea of checking it out meant as we made our way slowly down the cliff to the shingled beach below. We followed an animal trail down to the shore, watching our feet for signs of recent footfalls. The snow faded off the pebbles here but the snow-laden clouds on the horizon promised more to come and I didn't relish being out on the open sea in this weather.

What's this?" Arch asked, shuffling something in the shingle with his boot. He stooped to pick it up. He showed it to me. I turned the shiny metal piece around in my fingers, then realized what it was.

"It's them," I said. " A horse's bit. It's come off the harness of one of the horses. They came this way. Wait here." I shoved the piece back into his hand and ran toward the cliff's edge, where we had just descended. In minutes I melded with the cliff. Now I could investigate what had passed here.

The days turned to night and back again in my vision, then the sound of horse and cart reached my ears. I looked for it. There. At the far end of the beach, where there was no cliff. They came down to the shore. The whole company of demons, just as I saw before and the black coffin resting on the cart.

I scanned the shores for a boat, but there was nothing there. That was lucky for us. Perhaps they were delayed at the beach, waiting for one. We shouldn't be far behind then. My heart raced as I suddenly saw the coffin vibrate dramatically. The horses shied a little and the demons cursed. The cart stopped at the shore, but the coffin shifted again. She was alive! Relief washed over me like a waterfall and if I could speak, I would have cried with joy.

But what's this? A large demon stepped off his horse and went to the coffin, hissing. The creature placed a taloned hand upon it and instantly, a green gassy substance was emitted from his hand onto the coffin, snaking its way through a previously unseen air hole on top. The coffin stopped moving as the gas reached inside. So that's how they overpowered her. His horse got wind of it and reared, wild-eyed, and broke his bit and it dropped to the ground, unseen.

The demon ignored the horse and blindfolded them all before walking towards the shore, joining another like him, staring out to sea. My ears hurt as the two screeched the most piercing noise possible. I feared I had burst my eardrums it was so bad. Their heads tilted skyward, and their knees bent, they screeched once more, a long, drawn-out screech. What I saw next rendered me speechless.

The ocean before them opened like the mouth of a whale, just in front of where the two demons stood. It remained open as they grabbed their horses. The Demon cursed at the loss of his bit and threw a rope around the horse's neck instead, leading him forward to the opening. The cart rolled along behind them into this sea cave with the mounted demons following in its wake. When the last rider had entered this magical opening, the ocean closed behind them once more. It looked like a normal seashore once again. I was astounded.

"You're not going to believe this," I said as I walked back to my two colleagues.

"So, what are we going to do?" asked Patience, eyeing the cold sea, the wind whipping her red hair into her eyes. I pressed the spot of ultramarine on my hand and withdrew the Key. I knew I could open the ocean with it, but how long would it hold? We might have to travel far, so I drew out the Stone of Power once again.

"I will use these," I said. "The Ultramarine Key will open a passage into the Ocean for us. But I'll use the Stone of Power as well, to create an air sac whilst we are down there, just for insurance. It should hold power over the ocean just as much as other elements so I will give it a try. What have I got to lose?"

"Of course, it's sure to work." Arch said. "Its powers over the elements are legendary. We might get lucky and catch up with those demons finally." He did that thing with his eyes that scares me, and I look away, I know it's just his reflex, but still, it's disconcerting.

The three of us stood at the water's edge, where I told them I'd seen the demons enter the sea. I held the stone out on my palm and began the invocation of power once again, as the waves lashed at our feet. In the other hand I held forth the Ultramarine Key, pointing at the area I wanted to open.

With a rush of water, the ocean parted before us, like a portal, but more dramatic. We stepped into the gap between walls of water, rising higher above our heads as we went further in.

"This is so cool." Patience's fair face beamed at me as we entered our newly created tunnel into the ocean. The water closed at our backs, surrounding us completely, but left us inside an air sac for several feet around us, an air bubble to breathe in and keep dry as we walked further in. Without the stone, to follow would be impossible.

As we entered deeper water it got very dark, so Patience took out the Orb of Light and called forth its illumination. It was a powerful light that enabled us to see far into the distance all around us. Unfortunately, it also had other attributes. It attracted every living creature in the ocean that saw its glow.

"Oh heck... I hope this bubble holds." I whispered, as a pair of huge sharks came weaving towards us, their dead eyes trained on us. My legs wobbled a bit as they sped up, seeing us walking in their realm. We halted, waiting to see what would happen. But Patience held a hand out and began to make strange noises that sounded like gibberish to me. As soon as she spoke, the sharks stopped where they were and listened to her voice. Yes, they really were listening.

They approached more slowly, their eyes staring at Patience as she kept on speaking and waving her hand slowly from side to side. They waited, inches from the edge of the water bubble, taking in her every sound. Suddenly, they bolted, straight back to where they'd come from, leaving behind a few curious smaller fish, staring at us benignly.

"They won't come through now." Patience said. "They just wanted to see what we were. I did find out from them though, that the demons with the cart have headed towards the Pirates' Locker, which is in the deepest waters, a great chasm, miles further on."

"You found... You ... communicated with the sharks?" Arch asked wide eyed. Patience smiled.

"Yes, you of all should know that one of my skills is the ability to communicate with the world's creatures. Very useful at times. Shall we move on?" Arch visibly blushed at forgetting her skill, it wasn't what attracted him to her I guessed.

With Arch recovering from his faux pas, we headed on in our bubble tunnel, ever deeper into the ocean depths. Specks of luminous colours darted about on the periphery, and I wasn't sure if they were fisheyes or algae, but they were a bit spooky. I just hoped they didn't belong to some flesh-eating creatures like piranhas.

"I don't suppose they told you exactly where this Pirate Locker is did they?" I asked. "No, they just told me to keep going straight for a day and a night."

Arch and I groaned. The thought of trying to sleep in this bubble brought forth visions of drowning, not to mention being eaten alive by some dreadful monster as we slept. I prayed the stone held true and kept us alive in our little tunnel of air whilst we slept.

Curious-looking creatures of all sizes inspected us as we plodded on through the ocean. Sometimes we passed shipwrecks almost entirely encased in marine life. Other times we had to wade through fields of wet seaweed, almost as tall as ourselves. I wondered how on earth the cart and horses made their way through this. Perhaps they had some magic to keep it at bay?

A huge stingray followed alongside us for half a day, then flapped away losing interest after seeing nothing interesting happening. A shoal of spotted fish kept vigil in our wake, curious to see where we were going. I didn't mind them, their luminous blue tails were like fairground lights behind us, to cheer us on.

Before long, it darkened considerably and we realised it was night, several hundred feet above us. Somehow, I did not feel so tired on this first day of the ocean journey and both my colleagues felt the same. So, we plodded on in the company of strange looking jellyfish for a few more

41

hours, some bigger than us. Elsewhere, with the sea bed descending, we saw see-through fish, their scales very pale as though they sickened for something.

"What's that ahead?" Arch asked, his piercing eyes focused ahead. I peered into the murky depths before us and just beyond the glow of the orb's light, a dark outline of something huge began to materialize. It was oddly shaped and the closer we got, the more we realized how huge it really was.

"A large shipwreck." Patience said, eyeing the ancient canons barnacled on the sandy floor below it, with an array of treasures strewn about the ocean bed. Perhaps they had lain there for centuries, enjoyed by the sea life alone. "It might be a good place to rest for the night. Shall we take a look?"

We found a large gash in the side of the ship through which we could enter and found ourselves in a cargo hold. Several wooden barrels still sat clustered to one side, amid ropes and weights and sails. I wondered what they held. Alcohol probably. Anyhow, it was likely of no use to us.

"Thankfully, it is quite sheltered here from the sea creatures' curiosity. We might as well rest for the night as you said then," I said, touching the stone in my pocket to make sure it could not drift away whilst I slept and drown us all.

With parts of the cargo hold now emptied of water by our air sac, Arch sat on a barrel to eat, and I did the same. We realized that now the barrels were in our bubble we could check what was inside. Arch stuck a knife in the side to allow the liquid to leak out. Patience caught some in the horn and dipped a finger in the red liquid.

"Ugh! It's sour. Red wine at one time, probably the finest. Oh well. We'll make do with what the Horn offers us."

After our supper, we lay on the boards to sleep, but my mind wandered as the sounds of creaking wood and swishing creatures outside kept me awake. I opened an eye in the night, to find another eye peering at me, inches away, all menacing and dull. I jumped up in alarm but realized it was an eel, peering at me out of a large empty barrel in the watery section of the hold. I moved a few inches further away. Arch and Patience were sleeping peacefully, back-to-back, regardless of the many sounds surrounding us.

I rested my head on my pack and tried to see Brava in my mind, but all I saw every time was the blackness of the coffin. How could she still be alive in there? I knew she had an air hole, but did they feed her? Give her water to keep her alive? I worried until I could think no more. Darkness took me in the end, thankfully.

Chapter 4

The Stone held. We set off once again, refreshed after our food and rest. We jumped off the ship and floated down to the seabed in our bubble of air. We walked on, creating a trench in the deep sand as we walked. I wondered if the deep sand had slowed down our cart. I hoped so. We were grateful for the Orb as it was pitch black all around us, so deep were we that no sign of daylight reached us from above.

We were followed by luminous creatures wherever we went, but any that became too curious were quickly dissuaded from coming too close by a few words of gibberish from Patience.

After two hours walking, the ground became unstable.

"What's happening here?" Patience asked, eyeing the shifting sand. Bubbles rose from emerging cracks in the ground around us.

"Is it me, or is it getting warmer over here?" I asked.

Arch became agitated. "We need to move away from here quickly. I think it's ground movement from an earthquake. It might have created cracks in the earth's surface, allowing hot gases to come up from below- from the world's centre perhaps. Let's run."

We saw it straight afterwards, as we ran for our lives. Bright orange lava rose to the surface of the sea bed, along cracks opening up along the length of the deep bowl we were in. The ocean bubbled around us, sending gases bubbling through the depths. The fish scattered around us, moving away from the fissure that was rapidly opening behind us. Some didn't make it and flopped on their sides, immediately overcome by the hot gases.

We kept on running, hoping the bubble could keep up with us. It did. Arch used his great strength and grabbed us both and used his talent to jump great distances to get us out of the danger zone.

"Oh, my gods!"

We stopped abruptly as we teetered at the edge of a deep chasm in the ocean floor. It was so deep we couldn't even see the bottom and it stretched far out in front of us.

"What do we do now?" Patience asked, her face lined with fear.

"Can your orb cast a light down there do you think? If we could only see how deep, it is..."

"I don't know. If I dropped it in there, I'm sure it would, but it would mean we'd be in total darkness ourselves." She looked afraid for the first time since we started.

"No, we won't do that." I assured her. "There must be some other way."

We began to think what to do when a sudden though came to Patience. "I know what to do," she said. She cast her eyes around us, looking for something. "I need to find a ground feeder..."

Not quite understanding, I asked, "A ground feeder? What do you mean?"

"A creature that can withstand the deep pressures of swimming at great depths. It- oh, I see one. Wait a moment." We watched as she used her skills of communication once more, to call forth a large, white scaled fish that was emerging from the abyss below us. It came meandering towards us as Patience jabbered away. She delved behind her and drew out the small net that usually held the Horn of Plenty to her pack. She freed it and placed the Orb of Light in the net instead.

The fish stayed close to our bubble as Patience attached the netted orb around the fish's body. She talked continually to the fish until it made off into the abyss with the orb.

"What did you just do?" Arch asked, a worried look on his face.

"Don't worry. The fish will take the orb to the bottom for us, then come back up to return the orb."

"You are joking, aren't you?" I asked.

"No. She was quite happy to do it. Let's watch."

Unbelievable. But we watched as the orb journeyed further down into the abyss on the pale fish. The light revealed startled creatures, scuttling away from the light as it approached them. Deeper and deeper, it went, carrying on at an impossible depth, slowly taking the orb further and further away from us.

"It's so deep! Does it even have a bottom?" Arch asked, astounded. Suddenly, the orb jerked violently. "What's happening?" I asked, seeing the orb disappear completely now.

"Oh no! I think our fish has just been eaten by something. It's swallowed the orb too..."

We were in total blackness, and we began to panic. There was no way we could find our way without a light to guide us.

"Oh, look!" Patience pointed deep below, as the orb appeared again seconds later.

"It must have spat it out." Arch said. The orb dropped further and further until we could see it no more. Our hearts sank. Our fish wasn't coming back, and the orb was making its way to the bottom of this abyss.

"What do we do now?" Patience asked, feeling guilty at having used a flawed plan.

We jumped, holding hands, to make sure we kept together in the bubble, hoping we'd drop close to where the orb now rested. The dark waters here held strange-shaped creatures which I never knew existed in this world. They came near our bubble, the only hint of their approach being the spectacularly intense luminescence of their bodies.

The heat of the crevasse we left behind had dissipated. Perhaps we were moving away from it. I certainly hope so. I don't fancy being boiled alive down here.

We drifted ever downward, not knowing how fast or how deep we fell. It was surreal, not knowing our position in the world. We could have been upside down for all we knew.

"What if another creature's eaten the orb?" whispered Patience. The thought had crossed my mind and I rapidly threw it away. It would perhaps be game over, if that were to be the case.

I sensed something coming towards us. "Do you feel that?" I asked. My senses were pinging with impending danger. "Oh no.." Patience gasped in fear.

"What is it? What do you-" My words froze as Arch drew the Sword of Glass out of its sheath. I did the same with my own, trying to make sense of the darkness all around me.

Something touched my arm, something wet and clinging. Arch's sword was heard slicing through the air, and I felt liquid run down my arm.

"Hey, watch out, I'm here you know." I gasped, ducking. We decided to stand back-to-back for safety's sake. "Sorry-" He lunged his blade forward hitting something huge, its tip piercing some enormous creature that was trying to invade our bubble space.

"What's there?" I asked Patience. She had gone very quiet after her initial remark. "Can you communicate with it?"

We were tossed around in our bubble as whatever it was grappled with us, half in and half out of the water.

"I can, but it doesn't want to know. It wants its own way... I think it's a giant octopus."

The light suddenly appeared from somewhere below us, illuminating our situation. There it was, its tentacles almost totally engulfing our bubble. An evil looking beak opened as it coiled towards our bodies to draw us in for a feast. Arch and I slashed the creature's tentacles now that we could see what we were doing. But it was difficult to fight as we continually dropped. Pieces of tentacles fell to the ocean floor below us and the water inked up around us, making it hard to see again.

Patience fired one of her arrows into the creature for good measure and the combination of all our efforts finally killed our foe. It released its grip upon our bubble as it drifted off into darkness once more.

The orb lay still, the net half eaten by some creature. It had reached the bottom below us and we finally drew down to land beside it. All of us were relieved beyond measure to have retrieved it once more.

"Next time you have a brilliant idea, think again." I grinned to Patience. She grinned back and nodded and held onto her prize gratefully.

The chasm was so deep and truly enormous in width. It seemed endless in the dark. "Now what?" Arch asked.

I touched the water beside me in the hope of a vision. Nothing of course. I crouched down to touch the seabed and almost immediately began to see images pass before me, for which I was grateful. I straightened once more.

"We go this way." I said and headed left, along the bottom of the abyss. The creepy and oppressive walk was to last for another two hours before we saw anything new.

"Look at them all!" Arch said, taking in the numerous carcasses of shipwrecks from ancient times, lying in a jumble before us. "They must stretch for miles along the bottom of this chasm." Their awkwardly leaning broken masts stuck out randomly along the ocean floor and skeletal remains entwined in floating ropes were seen upon a few of the broken decks. Some rested amongst the treasures of the ocean floor, their skeletons dressed in gold and pearls, weighing them down.

"This must be the Locker," I said. "It's the graveyard of all doomed sailors and their ships."

"There are hundreds of them..." Patience stared at their pathetic treasures, clusters of coins and jewels almost obscured by the sandy bed and encrusted with barnacles. Lying to rot for the rest of time.

"How do we know which way to go?" she asked. I pointed.

"I think those faint lights far ahead might be the clue. It looks like a sort of entrance to something."

She looked from the distant swaying red lights back to my face. They hung between a group of wrecks lying together, from what we could see. We made our way towards them, wondering how they could glow like that, underwater.

"Those lights must have special power to be alight down here, a bit like our orb maybe?" Patience said. "Let's hope that whoever they belong to doesn't have such power too."

 We approached them an hour later. Merry voices and music came from somewhere within the circle of shipwrecks. Patience dimmed the orb and we watched from a safe distance as the party lights danced in this impossibly deep abyss. Then we saw them. Scores of figures dressed in gilded blue and black robes, their tricornes looking the worse for wear and many sported scars or missing limbs. They moved as though unhindered by the water.

"Pirates do you think?" asked Patience.

"Long dead pirates if they're down here," I said.

"They're armed." Arch pointed out the scabbards, swords and pistols, handing from their belts.

"Fat lot of use those pistols will be down here," I said. "But the swords could be a problem... Can either of you see the cart?"

We moved to look from different vantage points, circling wrecks nearby, but there was no sign of the coffin or the cart.

"Wait. Over there..." Arch pointed to a shadow moving upon the foc'stle of the largest ship. "Isn't that one of the demons you described? But I don't see a horse."

I looked carefully as the red light caught it in its sway. "Yes, you're right. It does look like one of them. Perhaps the others are inside the wreck with the coffin?"

We watched despondently as the many ancient pirate figures laughed and danced and drank from their golden tankards.

"How on earth do we get to find out? We don't have enough manpower to fight so many." Patience touched her bow by reflex.

I leaned on a canon to think, weighing up our options.

"Could you blend with the water or the sand to make your way over to see inside the ship?" asked Arch.

"I can't move within a blend. Only if what I blend with is moving, will I be able to move too and there's no guarantee it will take me to where I want to go."

"Oh, I see. How about your vision? Can you see the coffin with it?"

"I've been trying to do that since we came down here, but I don't seem to be able to see it at all. Maybe it's because we're under water or in the bubble, I don't know."

"Well, what do we have with us that might be useful then?" asked Patience, pulling out her artefacts.

"My Sword of Glass of course, will kill anything underwater. But I can't hope to kill all those by myself."

52

Arch sighed and sat on the canon. He suddenly thought of his shield. "We could hide under my Shield of Darkness, make our way over?" His face brightened.

"That's true," I said. "But I would still prefer it if there were far less of them over there. They might crash into us in our bubble, shield or not, then we'd be in trouble."

We sat a moment longer thinking. Patience's artifacts were no real help currently. Her bow and arrows would be useful should we need to fight, but we needed to be rid of several pirates first. I dug my hand into my pocket and felt the stone and shell in there.

"The Stone could muster up a storm, but that won't help us." I tucked it back and pulled out the Shell of Echoes and looked at it, hoping for inspiration. A smile found its way upon my lips.

"I know what to do," I said.

We practised a few examples before putting it to the test with the shell. Arch's booming voice was the best for it, we voted. He boomed into the shell, in his scariest voice.

"I have come to claim my gold and destroy all those who dare to touch my treasures. Beware, the end is upon you all..." He angled the shell towards the way we had come, so that the voice would reverberate from somewhere much further back. Then we got as close as we dared to the ship, using our Shield of Darkness to hide under.

When we heard the first echo, even the three of us were scared. It sounded so menacing and real. I had goosebumps on my skin as it now echoed towards the pirates.

The merriment stopped instantly, as their eyes searched the ocean in the direction we had come. Again, the voice repeated in echo and the pirates scattered to take up arms, dropping their tankards in panic. They ran en masse towards the voice, and we smiled at our success. But Arch noted one thing.

"The demon has stayed behind." Arch said, pointing to the foc'stle.

"Well, we'll deal with him soon enough. Let's go." I urged. We ran under cover of Arch's shield, closer and closer to what we hoped was the Pirates' den. The sign "Davy Jones' Locker" was pinned above the hole in the side of the largest ship, upon where the demon stood, looking out towards the pirates. We headed straight for it, our hearts in our mouths.

The sound of the pirates rampaging through the chasm behind us spurred us on. It wouldn't be long before they suspected something. The opening loomed, a faint red light within beckoned. We crossed the threshold and entered a place that could not be real. We stared at our surroundings in disbelief. "What the hell just happened?" I asked, lowering my sword.

"Where did the water go? It's not possible!" Patience turned full circle, looking for answers.

"Look- the hole we came through- it's still ocean out there. But... How can this be so different?" Arch was stunned, as all of us were.

"Where are we?" Patience was still mesmerised by the change since we passed through the hole.

"We must have come through some kind of portal," I said. " A portal- It can't be anything else." I deactivated the bubble, no longer needing it.

We stared at the view before us, from the road upon which strangely, we now stood. We were situated high upon a mountain, looking upon numerous other high peaks, undulating out before us, like the ridges on a dragon's back. Where are we? It doesn't look familiar at all. I took in the cold air. Snow lay all around us and began to fall anew upon the track that wound its way along the side of the mountain. I could see pieces of it wending its way down below us, between tall rocks that now and then, stood at the side of the road. There was no sign of demons or Brava's coffin, and we could see for miles from where we were.

"Can you tell which way to go?" Patience asked, her bewilderment evident. "I hear no cart or horse sounds."

Patience's incredible hearing was one of her skills and I did not doubt her.

I touched the track upon where we stood and melded with it. Clear images of the cart and horses came almost instantly. I got the impression we were not far behind them, but where were they? No current sign of them was to be seen by any of us.

"They went up the mountain and they're not far in front of us." I said, pointing up the track. "But we should be able to see them we-" I fell to the ground in sudden pain, crumpling in on myself, unable to finish the sentence. Screams and shouts filled my mind and terrible images flitted through my sight, the like of which I thought never to see. My arms hurt terribly for some unknown reason.

Patience's long red hair came loose and drew down in front of my face like a curtain, as she crouched before me, worried about my sudden agony. Her gentle hand touched my arm and I immediately felt less pain. I looked at her face.

"Better?" she asked. I nodded numbly. "How did you do that?" I asked. "Numb the pain, I mean." She just smiled and helped me up. Of course, one of her talents.

"What happened? What did you see?" Arch asked, his tattooed forehead lined with worry.

"It must be Brava. Something bad's happening to her. I saw her screaming in agony, surrounded by dark cloaks.

Their faces drained of all colour. This is the worst thing that could ever happen. But why would it happen now- with so many miles covered, why here, why now? But before I could even say any more, something else disturbing happened before us.

Chapter 5

We stepped back involuntarily, wondering if our minds were playing tricks upon us. Was this a hologram? A hallucination? We were on land, breathing fresh air again. The sea was nowhere to be seen.

"What the-?" Arch began.

"Are you real?" Patience asked, her hand stretching forward to touch the apparition. But Grinder didn't reply, instead he darted forward toward us, a frown embedded on his brow. He did not look happy- which was usually the case- his body armed to the teeth and his face even more frightening than usual. I drew my sword instinctively, from my past encounters with him, but he held his hand out to stay my hand.

"Thank the gods I found you!" Grinder said breathlessly. "Where the hell have you been for the past week? I couldn't find any of you at all until now."

"A week? It's only been a few days- We were under the ocean." Arch said simply, moving a step forward and turning his head as if to see where the ocean was behind us. "What are you doing here?"

Grinder drew a breath and looked beyond us momentarily. "Please tell me you've found Brava. We need her."

"Not yet, but we're close on her trail." I replied, without disclosing what I felt just before. "Why? And why aren't you protecting Gardia with the others?"

"It's a long story. We'd better talk as we walk. Where is Brava then?" He looked around us, twisting his head to scan the terrain.

"She's entombed in a black coffin, carried on a cart by demons on horseback and they're headed that way." Arch pointed. "Come tell us while we walk. Hopefully, we will catch up with them soon."

"Demons? Are you sure? So, he let them get into... Oh no. Now it makes sense."

"What does?" Arch asked, his head towering over Grinder's as he stopped to face him.

"They needed Brava out of the way... Perhaps it was Axl they were after all along. Without Brava to protect her, she was left more vulnerable..." We were bewildered.

"What do you mean? The other Servants are there to protect Axl and so is Pinni. He wouldn't let her come into any harm. I know Brava's the best fighter among us, but still, she's only one among many," I pointed out.

Grinder shook his head and huffed impatiently and halted, raising his hand for emphasis. "You don't understand! None of you do. I didn't see it before, but with the three of you gone, as well as Brava, it was his ideal opportunity. I see it now." I also turned to face him, fed up with his riddles.

"Well, I wish we could see it! You're not making any sense. Who is he and an opportunity to do what?"

Grinder cursed, impatient to get on.

"Pinni of course. The conniving devil. He had us all fooled. And Shadow is helping him... And to think I was friends with him all this time and he'd been secretly plotting with Pinni to bring about a coup!"

"A coup? Pinni wants to take over from Axl? The Servants won't stand for that. They'll put up a fight. And the people of Gardia will have a say in it surely?" I was incensed.

"We Servants left behind have been trying to fight, but Pinni closed off the armoury with a spell and set his own private guards to block its use. I was the only one to think of it in time before he got to it. I brought out as many weapons as I could carry."

"I can see that." said Patience, eyeing his impressive array.

"Oh, this is only a fraction of it. I left the rest I had with the other Servants before teleporting. They have swords and shields, some bows, but Pinni's placed some sort of charm on the castle guards. The weapons don't have any effect, they bounce back off. I was lucky to be able to get out of there. Pinni's set guards on the Wall of Keys and the Cave of Artefacts, so nobody can use them."

"So, you used your skill to get here, leaving the others to fend for themselves!" I growled at him. "You coward!"

He gave a smug grin. "The others told me to go find you. I can teleport anywhere on land but for a long time there was no trace of you. But when I finally located you on Axl's Window on the World, I jumped. I hid the Window somewhere safe, away from Pinni. I couldn't see Brava on it though."

"It might be because of the black coffin. It's probably bewitched somehow." Arch said.

"How did you get to her Window? Surely it was guarded too?" Patience asked. Grinder gave another sly smile. "I teleported myself into her room. The stupid guards were outside the door luckily, not in the room."

"That's quite a useful tool you have there." Arch said, which inflated Grinder's ego even more.

"Yes. I guess I can be useful to you in finding Brava. Plus, I'm a better fighter than most Servants." He was cocky as usual, but he was right.

"Bar Brava and Arch." Patience added in challenge. His face lost its cockiness momentarily.

"I guess so. Time will tell."

"Do you think they've taken here in there?" Patience asked, staring at the cleft in the mountainside further up. Under my guidance we had climbed higher up the track in the mountain's slopes, weaving through dense woodland and arrived at this opening. We walked closer and peered in.

"It's wide enough to take horses." Grinder said, eyeing the height and width of the cave. "We should go in, take a look."

"Wait." Patience said. "Let Blender check first." She halted with Arch at the entrance, but Grinder made a face.

"What? Why should I let Mouse do the checking? I can do it myself."

Arch nodded to me, ignoring Grinder. "Go on Blender, do your stuff."

I walked over and touched the cave entrance, allowing my body to be absorbed into the rock. The last thing I was aware of was Grinder's face, looking stupidly at me as I disappeared into the rock.

"What just happened? Where's he gone?" Grinder demanded, pacing across the entrance, looking for me. In seconds, I re-appeared before him, making him jump backwards with fright. Patience laughed.

"They've gone in. Not long ago," I said. "There are more demons with the cart now. I counted eleven on horseback, plus the cart driver."

"Damn," said Arch, ignoring Grinder's questions. "I hope our weapons will work on demons."

"I'm sure yours will." I said, looking at the Sword of Glass. "Let's go."

Arch, Patience and I led into the large tunnel, carved out of the mountain, with the Orb of Light leading the way. Grinder, still baffled, brought up the rear, looking as though he was trying to figure out if I could teleport too. We let him stew, keeping him in the dark for now.

We slowly edged our way deeper into the mountain, the tunnel winding its way up and down in equal measures from time to time. After an hour's trek, Patience halted.

"I hear the horses and the cart. And water. " Patience said. I was grateful for her skill in hearing. "They can't be far ahead."

We invoked the Shield of Darkness, to be on the safe side as we made our way along. Indeed, further in, the tunnel began to open out, descending into a long wide cavern, with narrow rivulets trickling down some of the walls, forming a black lake at its base. A wide waterfall also cascaded into it on the left. We could see faint glimmers of blue light, where the Demons held torches to guide their way. Patience doused the Orb immediately.

"What are they doing?" Arch asked. We all hunkered behind the huge stalagmite that stood almost thirty feet high to our left. It was a good vantage point from the path, above the floor of the cavern. Even without the Shield, they could not see us in the shadows of the large structure. There were several of them at intervals along the cavern floor and many lethal looking stalactites protruding from the high ceiling above. It was reminiscent of a creature's mouth.

"That's a good question." I replied. "Why they would stop over there by that waterfall I have no idea."

"Shall I teleport closer to them, surprise them? I could cut them down before they have time to react." Grinder said.

"It's a good idea, but not until we can get ourselves into position a bit closer, so we can join you in the attack. There are many of them. We can go closer under cover of Arch's shield." Patience said. "They won't see us."

"That's a great idea," I said.

"Okay, sounds like a plan." Grinder replied. "But here- take this dagger, your bow is okay from a distance, but you'll need something close up to attack with too." He passed over a long slim dagger with a jewelled sheath to Patience. "It's tipped with dragon venom."

Patience was surprised. This was very unlike Grinder, but she accepted it gratefully. We three positioned ourselves under Arch's Shield of Darkness and it expanded to blot us into shadow as we walked further down towards the cavern floor.

Grinder watched our progress but even he would soon lose sight of us. He relied on his counting to approximate the time it would take us to get close enough to the demons. Then he would teleport.

Our cue to attack came when Grinder teleported amongst the demons, who were milling around the cart as though waiting for something.

"Ha! Die, you venomous filth!" Grinder swung into action immediately upon landing at the back of three demons. He cut through their scrawny forms before they could react and draw weapons. They fell to the floor, black blood pooling from their bodies.

Patience fired her bow straight through two bodies in her path as Arch hurled himself towards two demons about to strike. His strength was well known, and he swung them by their arms at great speed, hurling them against the rock face with a mighty splat. They caved in upon impact.

I cut down a demon as I revealed myself, using the Sword of Justice. The mere touch of it upon the demon's skin had him dropping to the floor stone dead. But another demon came from behind me, seeing me in time to draw his own weapon- a lethal looking pointed axe.

As I turned my head, his greeny grey skin glistened with glee as he readied to attack. His pointed grey teeth were revealed as he drew back his thin grey lips in a deadly smile. But I braced myself and held my sword forth ready for the attack. He lunged forward with a strike. But I ducked from his axe and tried to pierce his stomach but missed. Again, he came lunging forward, leering and drew his axe high in an attempt to cut me down.

I remembered one of Brava's moves in training and saw no harm in trying it out. I spun myself away from him, which confused him. Upon my return spin, I drew one leg up high and kicked his arm hard, dislodging the axe from his hand. I immediately followed up with a slash across his body with my sword. His face contorted as the steel of death split his body and he crumpled to the floor.

I had no time to rejoice or seek another foe, for to my horror, Grinder's demonic expression caught my gaze as he hurled his own axe towards me. Was he possessed? It missed my head by mere inches and when I turned to look where it landed. I got a shock, for immediately behind me, arms raised with sword in hand to strike me down, stood a large demon. He now sported Grinder's axe in his face, almost cleaving it in two. He dropped like a lead weight to the cave floor.

I turned in horror to face Grinder. "You were aiming at him, weren't you?" His face now held a smug grin.

"Of course. He would have killed you if I hadn't thrown that axe."

He walked over to retrieve the axe from the demon and struck yet another a few paces away, one of two that were battling with Arch. Arch promptly stabbed his remaining foe with the Sword of Glass, killing the otherworldly creature instantly. "Thanks." he said to Grinder.

The sound of death came from the last demon still standing, as Patience withdrew her fired arrow from his heart. A poisoned dagger Grinder had thrown at him also stuck out from the demon's side, turning the surrounding skin black. He fell onto it, next to the other victims. We had done it. We had defeated the demons holding Brava.

We ran to the huge black coffin that held our colleague. Arch tapped on the wood and called out her name.

"Brava, are you in there? It's Arch, we've come to save you." A faint muffled cry came from within, she sounded weak and exhausted.

"I'm here. But I cannot move... They've done something to my body, and I can't see in here. It's too dark. Can you get me out?"

Arch and Grinder searched urgently for a way to open the coffin, but there seemed to be no lock, no seal, not even a lid. It was one complete unit by all intents.

"It's good to hear your voice Brava." Patience said as the two searched for a way in.

"We can't find a way to open it." Arch said. "I think we might have to use an axe to break it."

"An axe? What if you hurt her?" Patience said worriedly. "I can enlarge it, give her room to move if necessary?" Grinder said. We nodded and he placed his hands on the coffin, and it gradually grew large enough for our purpose.

"We'll be as careful as we can." Arch replied, taking up one of the axes strewn upon the floor. "Are you ready Brava? We're going to start breaking it up with the axes to get you out."

"Yes." her weak voice came instantly. What had they done to her?

They attacked the coffin with the axes for ten minutes and hardly created a dent in it. It wasn't wooden after all, possibly a type of metal alloy, unknown to us.

"What shall we do?" Arch asked. "This isn't working at all. I daren't use my eyes on the coffin, I might cut through Brava too."

"And Brava's going crazy in there with all the noise you're making!" Patience added. "We've got to find another way."

"We need something or someone that can transfigure objects. That might be a way to get her out," I said, thinking of what or who we had back at Gardia. I knew many of the skills our Servants possessed, but not all.

Grinder's face altered. His brows rose. " We need Veritas."

"Veritas? I asked. "Why?"

"His skills. One of them is the ability to transfigure objects. He would be ideal, only he's in Gardia, battling against Pinni and his cronies."

Before we could discuss how we could proceed, Patience froze as she heard something else.

"Something big is approaching. We need to get out of here!" Then we all felt its presence too, for our very skins raised in goosebumps as the air got colder. Something evil was approaching. Something big, for the ground reverberated with every step it took.

"There's no path wide enough for the cart to continue ... and we'll never get it back up the slope in time." Arch scanned the area for ways out.

"There's a couple of narrow tunnels over that way, but we'll have to leave the cart behind." Grinder said, looking around for ideas. "Where were they taking her then, I wonder?"

Arch lunged forward sheathing his sword and shield in place. "I'm not leaving her behind for whatever's coming! It's taken us all this time to find her. I'm not giving up." He mounted the cart and eyed the coffin quickly. "Come. Help me get the coffin into position on the end of the cart. I'm going to carry it."

"What?" Patience's eyebrows rose, her features incredulous. "You'll never be able to pick it up, let alone carry it!"

"Gee thanks." Brava's voice came from within the coffin, a slight levity in its tone.

"Sorry Brava, she didn't mean that. We haven't any time to lose. Quickly, lets slide it to the end so I can position it on my shoulders."

"My main ability is to support great weights. If Grinder can use his power of reduction to make it smaller, even better!" Grinder nodded and immediately placed his hands back on the coffin to reduce its size again for ease of movement.

The thought of him carrying the huge coffin, even if reduced in size, on his shoulders was ridiculous. I couldn't picture it, but still, we did as he asked, tying a rope to hold it in position over his shoulders. In seconds we had the coffin teetering on the edge of the cart's rear. Arch jumped down and positioned his shoulders under the coffin.

"Slide it and tie it onto my shoulders, quickly! That thing's coming closer. We're running out of time,"

It was true. A gigantic shadow of a horned being appeared at the far end of the cavern and with every step it took, the walls and floor reverberated. We hurried to do as Arch asked, our hopes pinning on this being possible.

"A little bit more to balance it... There. Yes. That's fine." Arch said as we slid the coffin in position. Brava kept as still and quiet as she could.

Arch, his hunched form, coffin perched on his shoulders, eyed us intently. "Lead the way, I'll be right behind you."

The wide-eyed expression on Patience's face said it all. We were all amazed at this feat. We hurried towards one of the tunnels ahead, Patience lighting the way with her orb.

Chapter 6

We'd gone only a hundred yards in when we heard an almighty roar of pure rage.

"I guess the horned giant has found the cart and bodies then." Grinder said, eyeing the dark tunnel behind. "We need to speed up a bit. Can you run at all Arch?"

"A little, for short spells at a time. Go ahead, I'll let you know when I need to take a breather." he replied.

"I wish we had a donkey or something. It'd be a great help right now," I said.

"You said you had the Horn of Plenty, Patience. Why don't you try to ask it for one?" Grinder said.

"Don't be ridiculous." She replied. "It's a living being."

"So? There's no harm in trying- unless you can think of something better."

Patience halted a moment, thinking about Grinder's words. "That's actually not a bad idea." she said. "I don't mean asking it for a donkey, but what about a barrow? The tunnels are wide enough for that at least, until we can figure a way to get her out."

"A barrow. That's what you came up with?" Grinder hissed with contempt. "I'd have asked for something better than that."

"Oh really? A donkey is not going to appear out of that, I can tell you now." Patience replied, giving him an even stare.

Patience concentrated on invoking the barrow and sure enough, we had a sturdy one placed in front of us a minute later. We helped Arch place the heavy coffin upon it.

"I really could have managed you know." Arch said.

"I don't doubt you, my love." Patience replied. "But if we met any resistance, we might need your hands free. This way it's safer, for now."

We hurried along as fast as the barrow would let us and soon, we were leaving sounds of the horned creature's ravings far behind.

"Do you think it will follow us?" Patience asked. I shook my head.

"No, did you see the size of its shadow? That thing's far too big to come through this tunnel. I think we're pretty safe for now. But if there are more demons in his wake, then we won't be safe for long."

The barrow worked well, despite the bumpy terrain. Arch handled the vessel well enough, his strong arms taking a lot of the pressure to avoid Brava being tossed about too much inside.

"This tunnel's endless." Grinder moaned after a long run through it. "It looks the same all the way along, never changing... And I swear I saw a stone with a crack in it just like that half an hour ago." He looked behind us. "You sure we're not going round in circles?"

We stopped; it struck a chord with us all. The tunnel was remarkably the same along its length, never changing.

"I have an idea," I said. I grabbed the axe I'd picked up off one of the demons and walked over to the cracked stone we'd all recognised.

"What are you going to do?" Arch asked.

"I'm going to carve a crude but recognisable shape onto this stone to mark it." I stepped back after three minutes to inspect my handiwork. The others stared at it.

"Okay, a triangle, fair enough. That will soon tell us if we're going in a circle or not. Let's go." Arch said, picking up the barrow handles once more. Onwards we went, with Patience's orb guiding our way. Our legs were aching with running on this uneven surface, but we had to keep on going. Half an hour later Patience stopped.

"What do you hear?" I asked softly, used to her keen auditory skills. She turned her head to face us, then held up the light upon the tunnel ahead. There was my mark, the triangle carved upon the stone ahead of us.

We slumped down to rest, despondent at our discovery.

"What's happened? Why have we stopped?" Brava asked.

"The tunnel is under a spell." I replied. "We seem to be getting nowhere, just going around in a long loop. I don't know how, but we seem to be stuck. There's no obvious sign of an exit. We passed no side tunnels."

"This mission is fast becoming a nightmare." Arch said as he rested with his back against the barrow. "I don't know if that creature spelled the tunnel or not, but nobody seems to have followed us in."

"Are any of the artefacts you have chosen any help to us?" Brava asked, her voice sounding frail from within. I went over to the air hole to speak to her.

"Brava, have they been giving you food and water since your capture?" I knew she wasn't the complaining type, so I had to ask.

"No, they gave me nothing."

"By the gods Brava! Why didn't you say so?" I asked. "Patience get something that Brava can drink and eat from the Horn, will you? She needs her strength."

"Oh, I'm so sorry Brava, I didn't think." Patience replied as she hurriedly thought of what best to give her under these circumstances. "This might work." She brought forth a flexible straw attached to a container of water and came over to the air hole to speak to Brava.

"I have some water for you here Brava. I will pass the straw down through the hole. See if you can position it in your mouth, then you suck up some to drink."

She was grateful for the water and soon her voice began to return to its normal tones, which was reassuring to us all. I wondered very much what was pinning her down inside that coffin, given how strong she was. Patience proceeded to give her some soup to suck bit by bit, to try and bring some strength back into her body. Seeing as we were going nowhere, we rested while she ate.

After resting and thinking about what to do, I stood up again as Patience put away the cups we had drunk from. We had taken a food break whilst we waited for Brava to eat.

"I know what to do," I said. Eyes looked in my direction, a grain of hope in their expressions. "I have the Viridian Key. I can get us out of here."

"Of course! Why hadn't I thought of it before." Arch smiled, tapping me on the back. "You made some good choices you know." I smiled back. "I did, didn't I?"

I brought forth the Viridian key from my palm and it glowed in my hand as I invoked its power. Holding forth the key in the direction I wanted to go, the glowing key emitted its strange beam of light and began cutting into the wall beside us. The others waited patiently as the earthen wall opened up, creating a wide new tunnel for us, one that I hoped would get us out of this mountain in one piece.

The key dimmed once more, its job done, and I replaced it in my pocket. "Shall we go?" I asked, turning to the others. "Then hopefully we can think of a way to get Veritas here to help Brava somehow."

The new tunnel did eventually bring us to the surface, and I was relieved to see that it was nowhere near where we had entered the mountain. We all hoped that the horned giant was far away by now.

We stood about two thirds of the way down a forested mountain, with no obvious signs of a path. There were mounds of snow clustered against rocky outcrops here and there and I drew my cloak over my shoulders now we were outside.

"What do you think the demons were going to do with you Brava?" I asked as we walked along in the bitterly cold mountain air. More snow threatened in the distance, with heavily laden snow clouds looming.

"I don't know, all I heard were the odd word I could understand now and then. I don't know what tongue they were speaking. I heard the words waterfall and icicles, but that's about it."

I wondered whether it had anything to do with the waterfall inside the cavern at all. I hadn't taken much notice of it before, but the cart rested only twenty yards away from it. Perhaps they intended to do something with it?

"Well, now that we're in the open again I can teleport back to Gardia to see if I can find Veritas," said Grinder. "I hope to hell he's managed to stay clear of Pinni all this time."

"Hopefully I'll see you soon. Be careful. Don't get caught." Grinder said, moments before he disappeared.

I turned to the others. "We need to find somewhere to shelter for the night. It's going to be snowing, but I'm not going back into that cave."

We scanned the darkening valley in the hope of spotting some shelter we could take. It was densely forested around us, but there was the odd gap in the trees now and then.

"No sign of huts to shelter in. I guess we'd better make our own." Arch said. "I can weave some branches to form a shelter for us, cover them with undergrowth to keep us dry."

"Sounds good, but I have a better idea," I said. "Let's get off this steep part of the mountain first."

We made our way slowly further down the mountain, deliberately keeping off any tracks we'd taken up before. It was too risky. We found a suitable animal track to follow and ended up in a sheltered hollow lower down in the foothills. It was a perfect spot to keep us dry. Large evergreens made a wall of defence at our backs and their low branches were ideal to weave other branches onto, to create a shelter. A miscellany of other trees and shrubs grew at the front of the hollow, which made a perfect screen against intruders.

Although Arch was skilled in weaving wooden saplings, I decided to use the Stone of Power to help create a suitable shelter. In no time at all we were all settled under a woven dome covered by undergrowth, save for a hole to allow smoke from a fire to dissipate out. It would not be seen in this weather and besides, the evergreens were far too tall for it to be spotted.

Soon we were cosy around our fire, the domed shelter warm and safe from the increasing snow outside. I was glad, for it would hide our own tracks. We had plenty of head height inside and the space accommodated Brava's coffin with ease. We placed her close to the fire to keep her warm. Arch threw his own cloak over her coffin as an added warmth.

"Arch, you're going to freeze without that." Patience said, eyeing his cloak. He only had his leather jacket otherwise. He grinned coyly. "Well, I had in mind another way to keep myself warm actually." He went to sit closer to her.

"Oh really?" Patience's lips curled up at the sides. I guess I must have missed something.

"It's a good shelter. Thank you Arch for the idea." I said, passing him a plate of some bread and cheese from Patience's offerings. She'd procured us some brandy as an extra to keep us warm through the night. Now that we could feed Brava via a straw, she became more of a part in the conversation, as her strength returned. The brandy might help her too, in more ways than one.

She told of the day she was taken. Her food or drink had been drugged and in her unconscious state she was taken somewhere. When she woke up, she was inside this coffin. I felt her pain. It would be too claustrophobic for me to be inside there like that. I shuddered at the thought. Worse still, what if she needed the toilet? I tried to put that one out of my mind quickly.

I had previously seen visions of limbs being hacked, and I wondered if this was why Brava couldn't move. I didn't dare ask her in case she panicked inside the coffin. I would not dare to bestow that thought on her.

As we rested on our bed rolls upon the soft fern undergrowth, we talked of the situation back at Gardia. I noted that Patience had incorporated Arch into her own cloak as they lay side by side on their bedrolls. Grinder had not told us where Pinni had taken Axl or how she was taken. It was extraordinary, given that she possessed an ancient magic that she could have fought them with. It worried me as I lay on my back, until I eventually fell asleep from exhaustion.

"No! Don't. You can't do that. Please!" I cried, pleading them to stop, but they did it anyway. The blood flowed everywhere, soaking the floor. It was like a crimson pool in the firelight, slowly ebbing out of her body, draining her of life. My body quaked as I sobbed. My shoulders shook with sadness. Then a voice called me.

"Blender, wake up! You're having a nightmare." It was Arch, crouched over me beside the fire. The images I'd seen moments ago faded into shadows. Where was I? Then I remembered.

"Sorry, was I calling out?" I drew myself up on my elbow and glanced towards the coffin and Patience, her cinnamon hair splayed about her face as she slept peacefully. "You didn't wake the others thankfully- just me." he said. "Well, Patience was... Rather tired. " He blushed. "Was it a vision?"

I sat up, rubbing my eyes and whispered, so the others couldn't hear me."I don't know for sure. I hope it was just a nightmare. If it was something real, then we're really up to our necks in it! All of us."

He leaned closer. "What did you see?" I contemplated whether I should tell him all of it or just some of the details. I opted for the latter.

"I saw lots of blood and Axl dying. I'm sure it was just a nightmare though. Probably brought on by what Grinder said. Let's get back to sleep while we can. It's still the middle of the night." I lay my head back down, hoping Arch would do the same. There was no need to panic. We could do nothing about it.

"Yes, you're probably right." said Arch. "Good night."

It was still cosy when I woke in the shelter. The inside had taken on a blue-green tone, from all the snow reflected all around us I presumed. Someone had made sure the fire kept going all night, otherwise we might have frozen.

Patience was already feeding Brava and talking softly to her. Arch was munching on toast and warming his feet by the fire. "Had a good sleep?" Patience asked brightly.

"Yes thanks, you?" She blushed and smiled, nodding.

"Some of the time, although I was worried about what was going on in Gardia for part of the night. I wonder how Grinder's getting on?"

A cold icy breeze wafted into our shelter, as a head popped through our makeshift woven cloth door." Talking about me?"

"Grinder! We thought you'd still be in Gardia.." Patience said, open mouthed. "Where's Veritas?"

He came in to warm himself by the fire, closing the woven door behind him. I caught a glimpse of deep snow outside, and I was glad we'd been inside here out of its chill.

"Any brekkie going? I'm starving." Grinder made himself comfortable and grabbed some of Arch's toast and coffee. "I'll get some more then!" Arch said, glaring across at the new arrival.

"Great shelter you've got here, couldn't have done better myself." He turned to look towards the coffin. "How's she this morning?"

Brava's voice replied clearly out of the coffin. "She is very much alive and can hear perfectly well thank you." He reddened and almost choked. "I hope you bring good news."

He swallowed the lump of toast and replied." Veritas will be here shortly. He didn't want to travel instantly like me. He's coming on a winged horse. Grace summoned one for him. That's one of her skills you know- she can summon any creature. Figured out what you're going to do yet?" He looked at us as though we were a magical solution to everything.

"Well, I would have thought that was obvious." I replied testily. "Ooh, get you, little Mouse." Grinder gave a cold grin. "Finding courage, are we?"

Patience cut in icily. "Blender has never lacked courage. You just don't see it, that's all. He keeps it well hidden. He's not boastful like you."

"Right." He replied just as icily and proceeded to grab some more toast that Arch had just newly prepared for himself. After a long silence, Arch asked, "What is the current situation in Gardia then? Where is Axl?"

Grinder looked grim. "We still can't find where they have taken Axl, but..." There was a long pause as he chose his words carefully. "There was a lot of blood on the floor of the Guardian's room. And I mean a lot. It looked like a bloodbath in there. I don't know if she's even alive still."

"She is, I feel it." I said, but my stomach roiled with realisation. "But I fear she has lost much more than blood. They have cut off her power. I saw it in a vision. They have cut her arms off."

Patience lunged to the side and vomited, her knees buckling under her. Arch went to support her, his own face grim. Even Grinder showed his human side for once and showed the effect it had had on him too.

"That's what I was afraid of." he said quietly.

Chapter 7

Arch was the first to spot them coming over the horizon, like bats in the grey, swooping towards him as he stood watch outside. "They're here." He called to us.

"They?" I asked from the interior.

"Yes, Veritas has brought five more winged horses with him- for us I presume." I wrapped my cloak around me and exited the domed shelter. Patience was feeding Brava as Grinder fed his face by the fire.

The flapping wings caught my ears as soon as I stood outside, then a soft whinny from one of the horses as they came in to land close by. They were magnificent creatures- taller than normal horses and much more powerful. They could read your mind when you rode on their backs, knowing exactly where you wanted to be taken without the need for other communication.

Little flurries of snow fell from some of the laden branches surrounding us, as their wings stirred the air upon landing. Their hooves hardly made a sound as they came to rest upon the pristine snow, but their nostrils flared with the effort of the journey. The whiteness of their breath showing in this cold atmosphere.

Veritas dismounted with a smile and hugged Arch, who was a close friend. Arch took the bunch of reins from Veritas' hand and tied them to branches nearby as Veritas brushed away the snow from his jet-black hair. The horses promptly sat in the snow to rest, closing their eyes calmly as they rested their heads tucked under a wing. I couldn't help but smile at their grace and beauty, despite their size.

"Thank you for coming." Arch said to his friend as Veritas tried to set in order his windswept hair. It was normally poker straight and not a hair out of place, in a fetching ponytail. "I didn't know you could transfigure objects." Veritas smiled and re-tied a leather thong to his man-bun to keep it tidy, the rest of his hair was left loose.

"Yes, you wouldn't know I suppose. Whenever we've both been together on a quest, I've never needed it. And the subject never came up." He smiled at me, noticing me standing by the shelter. "Hello Blender. I hear you are to be congratulated. Well done in finding Brava so quickly. It couldn't have come at a more opportune time. Things in Gardia are pretty bad I'm afraid."

His honeyed skin stood out against the surrounding snow, and I was jealous of his immaculate good looks. He was always kind to me. He removed his sabre from his back to sit. "Any news of Axl?" I asked, hopeful. I led the way into the shelter.

"No, nobody knows where Pinni has taken her, and his guards would shoot you sooner than speak to you about it. They're everywhere. I was lucky to get out. The others are planning to meet us in Grunwald, the East Forest upon our return. None dare risk staying in Gardia on their own now."

The shelter warmed again as Arch shut the door behind him and Veritas. I moved aside so he could warm himself at the banked-up fire, as he made immediately towards it, hugging Patience as she came to greet him.

"Nice shelter you've got here. I bet Arch wove the branches- he's really good at it." He smiled broadly and I saw for the first time how perfect his teeth were. He had elven ancestry, with high cheekbones and slightly pointed ears and his sense of balance was legendary. Everybody seemed to like him in Gardia. Well, at least they did before all this.

Patience gave him some hot coffee and a muffin, and he gladly accepted. "Thanks Patience. I can't remember when I last ate. Things aren't normal in Gardia, as you can imagine. There's no canteen or routine for us anymore. Only Pinni and his men get to eat these days. Everyone's just trying to survive- hiding out where they can." His

85

face darkened with sadness. "I just hope we're not too late to rescue Axl." A voice, level and strong came from the coffin. "Well, when you've warmed yourself up, perhaps you can get me out of here, then we can do something about it."

Veritas stared at the coffin and paused eating. "Sorry Brava. For a minute I'd forgotten you were in there. Just give me a couple of minutes to warm up will you?"

"Sure, I've got all day." Brava replied sarcastically.

He stood at the coffin, eyeing it from all angles. "And you say to tried to break it with an axe?"

"Yes, not even a scratch on it, as you can see." Arch said.

"You can sort it out though, can't you?" asked Grinder, watching from the fire.

Veritas knocked and tapped the coffin in various places then replied. "Yes, I think so. Okay, stand back everyone. Brava keep very still in there. I wouldn't want to transfigure you into the same thing by accident, okay?"

"You're kidding right? I can't move a muscle, only my head. Get on with it." Brava was anxious to be out of there and I couldn't blame her.

"All right."

Veritas placed his left hand on the coffin and closed his eyes, concentrating. Everyone watched spellbound, as he began his incantation in a low monotone voice. In seconds, his left hand began to redden, then glowed, slowly developing an orange fire glow that filled the space around it. It now spread along the black exterior of the coffin, turning it too into a glowing orange light.

 Veritas slowly waved his right hand above the left, his incantation increasing in volume. This brought about a distinct transformation in the texture and colour of the coffin before our eyes. The change lasted another minute and as the glow died down and returned to his left hand, the exterior of the coffin had changed. It was now made from woven flat reeds.

We heard Brava gasp dramatically as the glow finished. We hoped it was with relief.

"Are you all right Brava?" Patience asked, touching the new coffin surface tentatively.

"Yes, it's just so much lighter in her finally! I can see through gaps in the weave, and I can breathe better at last." Arch stepped forward with his dagger. "I'll slice it open along the sides with this."

"I'll help you. I'll use mine too." Grinder said, moving to the other side of the woven coffin. The sound of reeds breaking and coming apart was reassuring and we all watched, brows raised in hope, as the coffin top was cut away around its circumference with the daggers' edges.

"It's free!" A final crunch denoted the woven piece was released from its base. Grinder and Arch lifted off the woven lid to reveal Brava underneath.

"Oh my god!" Patience's eyes looked on in horror and we all stared in disbelief at Brava's predicament, now that the lid was removed. She could finally see for herself why she couldn't move. Her neck craned up to see her body and panic began to fill her eyes. But Veritas stepped forward to reassure her.

"It's all right Brava. It's not a problem. Don't worry. I'll soon have you out of there." he said, his arms outstretched above the body.

Brava's whole body, apart from her head, was encased in lead. It was moulded over her body, pinning her limbs so that she could not move. It was horrifying to behold, very much so for Brava herself and she imagined all sorts of horrors that had befallen her body underneath all this. No wonder Arch felt the weight despite Grinder's reduction skills.

"What have they done to me?" Brava cried; her eyes full of terror. I stepped forward to try and reassure her.

"It will be all right Brava. It has been placed there with magic. You have not been subjected to molten lead. You are not maimed, please believe me," I said.

She looked into my eyes, searching for truth in them, but it was Veritas who convinced her.

"He is right. And you know I can only speak the truth." He saw her slowly beginning to relax again, knowing it was why he was called Veritas.

Brava nodded, sighing with relief. "So, what can you do?" she asked. "Leave it to me. You should feel a slight warmth around your body, nothing to be alarmed about." He smiled, revealing his impeccable white teeth once again. Brava nodded.

"All right, you may proceed." she said, reclining her head once more.

Veritas repeated the process he had performed before, this time touching the metal sheet with his left hand. Again, it began to glow with the beginning of his incantation. It intensified in its luminosity as he continued. Everyone watched intently when suddenly, Patience's eyes darted towards the outer door.

"What is it?" I asked immediately. "There's something troubling the horses. I can hear the change in their stirrings." she said.

Veritas did not lose concentration but kept his transfiguration going. Patience's eyes met mine and I opened the door to the shelter and darted out, with Grinder and Arch on my tail.

We all noted the unease that had befallen the horses. They were rising from their rest prematurely, their eyes darting about. Patience came from behind Arch, leaving Veritas to it. She made a line towards the horses and touched their muzzles gently, each in turn, calming them with soft words as they made small noises to her.

She stared at us; brows knitted with worry. "There is something big approaching us. Something bad, they can feel it." We drew our weapons as Patience led the horses by their reins to a hidden niche behind our shelter, pacifying them with words of comfort as she went. They followed her without hesitation, their snickering dying down as they moved away. In moments she was at our side, her bow raised in readiness.

"I tied them securely." she said. "It's coming."

We moved further away, towards a section higher up on the mountainside to protect our shelter. It didn't take long for us all to hear it moving now, as trees creaked and snapped with its movement. It was enormous. We scuttled ever upwards, closer to the sounds, to see what was coming, crouching low for fear of being seen.

The first sight we got of the creature were the sharp points of its horns, high above the treeline ahead, like needles piercing the cold air.

"It's huge!" Grinder cursed. "That bloody creature from the cavern's found us!" It let out a mighty roar as it threw aside branches in its way, cutting a path through the dense forest before us. Immediately we ran to get to a good vantage point to attack this thing. Doing so wouldn't be easy, and there was debris being flung about everywhere by the horned giant.

"How the hell did it find us?" Grinder hissed.

Its fists could grasp entire tree trunks, so large was the creature and if you did not pay attention, you could be killed by just one random throw from the giant. For the first time I saw its head, poking out above the treetops as it plodded towards us.

My face crumpled with disgust as I saw its sheer ugliness. Its head was very bull-like, sporting a mucus riven snout bigger than my head, with an iron ring pierced through its nostrils, itself caked in mucus. It dribbled down its wide squat snout, causing rivulets of gunge to form all the way down past its beastly fangs onto its stout furry neck. The neck itself undulated in mounds of pure muscle and steam seemed to be bellowing out of its entire head.

I caught a glimpse of its giant ape like feet, tearing apart the trees to make room for his enormous bulk. They were slick with blood and gore. I wondered what poor creature met its end that way and I swallowed hard. It was a creature of Chaos I guessed. How did it get here?

Glancing across at the others crouched alongside me, I could also see the same disgust on their features too. None of us had seen anything as hideous as this creature before and it was heading directly towards our shelter. Did it know it was there? We had to act fast.

Patience's arrows were quickly unleashed and headed straight for the creature's heart, but he managed to flick them impotently aside. This was unheard of. The Bow of Hearts was supposed to have arrows that homed in directly on a creature's heart to kill it, no matter how bad the shot had been. In this case it had foiled them. Patience looked at us in despair. But she was not done. She moved position.

She was trying to get to the right flank of this creature, and I was under the impression she was aiming to try and score a hit from behind him, so he couldn't see the arrows coming. The three of us launched ourselves forward with a cry of battle to try to distract the creature so Patience could get behind him.

Grinder led the assault, hurling his battle-axe directly at the creature's leg to sever a tendon perhaps. But the axe bounced off the bull like creature's tough hide, leaving only a scratch and almost scalped Grinder as it bounced back towards him. He ducked just in time to avoid being decapitated.

Arch charged towards the giant to get a stab at his leg with the Sword of Glass. It was designed to kill creatures of magical creation, so he was confident he could kill him if he could only get near. I charged forward with the Sword of Justice at the same time, so one of us at least, might get a chance to get close enough to score a hit.

It caught sight of us in time to take a swipe at us with the branch in its grasp. We were both buffeted through the air and landed heavily in the snow several yards away, but we clung onto our swords, for our life depended upon it.

"Get the shield!" I yelled to Arch. It was still inside the shelter; such was our hurry to find this creature.

"I'm not leaving you." Arch shouted back. But Grinder had recovered from his shock and was now preparing to launch another assault on the creature.

"Go get it! I'll keep it distracted." Grinder said and he rushed forward, hurling a dagger he'd brought from the armoury at the creature. It sang through the air and pierced the giant's lower leg, dangling precariously at an angle. The giant roared with pain, which gave us encouragement.

Patience and I lunged forward straight away as it swayed in pain. Another hurl from his battle-axe and this time,

Grinder managed to slice a deep gouge in the giant's leg, just below the knee. It faltered, teetering on its legs in pain, roaring out in anger. His branch swiped Patience aside.

Arch returned, having jumped the great distance and we both shot forward together under the shield, dodging low sweeps from the branch it held, trying to swat us aside. It seemed to sense us despite the shield, which we found worrying. We were inches from its hairy hide, it was now or never.

Under the shadow of the Shield, we stabbed it in each leg with our swords and immediately it dropped its branch towards where we stood.

"Look out!" I yelled at Arch, seeing the tree sized branch heading towards him. But instead of moving aside, he threw the shield at me and held his arms braced above his head and caught the huge branch with both hands. I knew it must weigh a couple of tons by its size, but Arch held it easily, before lunging forward and dropping it on the creature's head.

Out of nowhere, a fierce battle cry jarred our senses and out of the corner of my eye I saw a flicker of something dark fly across my vision and hurl itself upon the creature's chest in front of us. It was Brava. She was much thinner than I remembered. But she clung onto the creature's hairy chest with one hand and repeatedly stabbed it several times in the throat with the sword Grinder had left for her. Ignoring the black, spurting blood that issued from its neck, splattering her ebony face, she kept up the momentum, yelling fiercely like a banshee until the giant's head toppled over onto its side, partly severed by Brava's vicious strokes. His body rolled over on its side with the slope of the hill.

As he turned, we saw Patience standing ten yards away from behind the creature, a wide smile on her face. It was then I noted three Heart arrows sticking out of the giant's back, right over his heart. Together, we had done it and we stared in disbelief for a few seconds at the fallen creature, then we whooped with delight, clapping each other on the back in congratulation.

Behind us, Veritas stood, clapping his hands, looking very pleased, with not a hair out of place.

"Well done you lot. I think he's dead now. Let's have some tea." He turned heel and made for the shelter, and we laughed, happy that Brava was with us once more.

Chapter 8

"So, all this has happened since I was taken?" Brava sat at the fireside, enjoying a proper mugful of coffee and a solid meal at last now that she was free of her coffin. The discarded wet moss with which she had washed away the creature's blood from her face lay at her feet. She kicked it into the fire where it sizzled and shrank.

Patience told her of our undersea adventure and discovered that Brava had felt no different in her coffin whilst in the ocean. "They must have placed a powerful spell on us all, to be able to travel into that chasm without suffering," she said. She laughed as Arch told her of his echoed message and told me it was a clever idea of mine.

Patience leant over to whisper to Brava privately, but Brava laughed out loud at what she'd been asked. She shared her answer without inhibition, to all of us. "You were worried I might need a pee? Of all things that could have happened to me, you worried about me needing the toilet?" She laughed heartily again, with Grinder joining in. Brava leaned over to reply, her voice back to normal and we all subconsciously craned our heads to hear. "I was paralysed in that coffin, I felt nothing from the neck down, so be assured, I didn't ever feel the need-thankfully!" Patience blushed but smiled and nodded her head.

I looked across to the transfigured affair in the corner of the shelter, noting Veritas had transformed the heavy lead sheet into a light blanket instead. Obviously, a good choice, easily tossed aside by Brava. I couldn't help but stare at her much-altered form as we sat around to give her time to regain her strength. It had been a long time since she had eaten anything decent. Her skin looked dehydrated, not its usual silky sheen.

"Yes, much has changed in Gardia." Veritas said, his face saddened. "I wish I'd foreseen Pinni's intent, maybe I could have prevented it all happening."

"None of us had any idea." Brava replied. "It was well hidden from us by Pinni's ancient magic, the conniving bastard. I don't even think your powers of enchantment could alter him Veritas."

She growled, her face full of anger. "Wait till I get back there; I'll kill him with my own bare hands." She glowered. "I don't think it will be quite so easy," I said. The three looked at me in surprise, having been unaccustomed to hearing me say anything in any of the Wheel meetings no doubt. Only Patience and Arch held no such surprise in their eyes, instead, they smiled, nodding in agreement. Brava looked at me intently then spoke to me softly.

"I don't think I have thanked you properly for coming out here to find me. From what I hear, you have had quite an adventure. They gave you a real run-around. You did very well to achieve your goal. Axl was very wise in choosing you."

The others took great note of anything Brava had to say as this was praise indeed, endowing me with a state of greater respect amongst my fellow Servants. They nodded in agreement. Only Grinder looked uncomfortable in doing so.

"Yes, Axl knew how clever he was and now more should appreciate it too. We all are in your debt Blender." Patience smiled. I blushed, unused to such praise.

"Axl had more faith in me than I did," I said. "Once I was chosen, I just gave it my full commitment. I'm glad it worked out but without Arch and Patience, I would not have succeeded."

"Nonsense. You are our equal." Arch said. "You played your part and we played ours."

"That is the truth of it." Veritas added. "But now, we all face an even greater battle, one against powerful witchcraft. I don't know if we'll be so successful in winning the next confrontation. But perhaps together we might stand a small chance."

Brava stood finally, her impressive height filling the headroom. She had eaten well in the last few hours, and it was certainly great to see her back on her feet again, her skin starting to take on that same old glow. And having fought with us whilst weakened was a feat of its own. I couldn't imagine any of us others able to do so. She is such a key figure amongst the Servants. Kind of like our backbone. We were highly relieved to have her back with us. But can we save Axl? Even with Brava, that may already be too late, if my visions are anything to go by.

"I think it's time we returned to Gardia my friends." Brava grabbed the weapons that Grinder had brought for her and strapped them to her belt. She looked at each of us in turn as she spoke. "We shall head towards the Eastern Forest. There we can plan what we need to do, before returning to the Corridor of Sighs. Come, let's waste no more time. Axl needs us."

We rode back towards Gardia on the winged horses, which was both exhilarating and frightening at the same time, if a little cold. We rode bare backed and only had the horse's mane to hang on to. I held on for dear life when my horse took a sharp dive to avoid storm laden clouds. I think I spent those downward sessions with my eyes screwed tight so I wouldn't see the sheer drop below. And I'm sure my horse lost several strands of mane hair as I grasped so tight.

The others seemed well versed with travelling this way, some hardly holding on at all. Grinder was waving his hands about in conversation with Arch as we sped along, oblivious to the drop below. Now and then, Veritas or

Patience would come close by my horse to check I was all right. I guess they probably saw the green colour of my face as I urged myself not to vomit all over the poor horse.

I couldn't help but admire its power though. Its strong velvety wings held great force with every flap. I could feel the lift each time it happened. Each impressive wing spanned twelve feet to its tip and if I should tumble onto one, I was sure of its ability to hold my body until I could get back into position on its back.

I was sure that Patience was communicating with Lightning- which was my horse's name. She was probably being helpful and telling it to ride smoothly for me. She's like that, very thoughtful.

Each horse had a different personality, she told me, and all were named according to their character. Mine was called Lightning because it was a fast and bright horse. Its silvery white hide would glisten in the sunlight, like a streak of lightning passing across the sky. Even in the grey snow-laden sky it shone brightly. I asked her what Grinder's horse was called, as it seemed to love dive bombing now and then, much to Grinder's amusement. "His name is Jester," she said, "which suits Grinder's temperament I would say." I laughed.

Brava rode upon a magnificent black stallion, which tossed its head back frequently, its tail swishing as it flew. Patience told me it was named Spirit. It certainly had plenty, enough to match Brava's own. They looked as if they belonged together, and I began to wonder if Veritas had deliberately made careful selections of steeds for us beforehand.

Through the dense grey cloud cover we saw land below us at last, as the horses swooped lower down through the grey, ready for landing. The vast Eastern Forest of Grunwald loomed ahead, blanketed in snow. It looked very different from when we first set off from it on our quest, and that seemed so long ago.

Spirit drew its head back sharply suddenly and made a huge racket. "What is it boy? What do you sense?" Brava patted its neck in reassurance.

She looked down at the forest below like the rest of us and we all saw what Spirit had sensed. We drew our horses back up at the same time, seeing the land below teeming with demons. Every clearing in the forest was littered with their moving armies.

"I hope our friends aren't amongst all those! Where did they come from?" Patience asked, her face grim. "I would guess our friend Pinni has summoned the forces of Chaos forth. He must think they will help him gain the power he requires." Veritas said. "It seems our job just got a million times harder."

"What do we do now? We can't land in the forest with the demon horde there." Arch looked to me as mission leader. It was Grinder that spoke though. He looked towards me, drawing the dappled grey Jester closer.

"What about your visionary skills Blender? Can you visualise where the other Servants are?" I stared back at him, taken aback by his words. It was the first time he'd called me by my name. But I nodded and gave it a shot, although normally, I must be quite still to visualise things away from my sight.

I closed my eyes and began to search through my mind. With every movement of Lightning's wing though, the tiny fragments I managed to latch onto would disappear again as quickly. I tried again, focusing harder.

"It's no use," I said. "The movement of the horse is stopping me from seeing properly. I need to be still to "See". I have to land somewhere."

We looked for any possible place where I could bring Lightning down without risk of running into the hordes of demons. Brava had the skill of Keen Sight, she could see much further than anyone and now, her amber eyes scanned the cloudy blanket below us for a possible landing site. In a few minutes, she found one.

"I see a place." She pointed slightly southward, where I could just about see a high rocky plateau standing out in the cloudy sky. "There are currently no demons that I can see there. We'll bring the horses down upon it, so Blender can use his gift to track them down.

We turned our horses towards the outcrop, flying high above the clouds, to avoid detection by the demon hordes. The wind was keen, and we held on tightly as we descended towards the rocky heights.

We cut through the clouds, the sleet and snow luckily holding back as we came in to land. The plateau stood high above the western end of the forest and low clouds hid the view of the horde infested trees below us. The wind whistled across the plateau, biting our skin and we rode our horses towards the shelter of a tall outcrop of rocks fifty yards further along from where we touched down. At least we would be out of the wind there as the rocks formed a vaguely horseshoe shape to protect us from the worst of the wind and sleet.

"It's much better here, the wind can't get at us," Arch said, bringing his grey stallion, Samson out of the wind's clutches. The horse soon settled himself down to rest on his haunches, along with the other horses, in the sheltered curve of the rocks. My body warmed within my cloak as soon as we were out of the cold wind, and I was glad that Brava had seen this place. It was high enough to be safe from the demons far below. I reckoned we were several hundred feet above the treetops here.

I had grown to like Lightning; she was placid and made little snorting noises when I patted her muzzle. She let me patiently lead her to shelter then sat down with the others.

"I'll make a fire as we rest awhile," Veritas said, gathering sticks laying around in the rocky alcoves. Patience opened her pack to get the Horn out as I looked for a good place to sit still to focus my mind. I spotted a dark niche under an overhanging rock nearby, well out of the weather, with dry grass and brushwood blown in, at my feet. A suitably shaped rock waited for me to sit down upon it.

As the other Servants created a fire and prepared some food and drink, I settled quietly on my rock and closed my eyes, drawing upon thoughts of our comrades left behind- Hope, Stretch, Pax, Grace and Causia. Shadow can go hang himself, the traitorous bastard.

My mind wandered through fleeting glimpses of demons running, some attacking, some falling. In a mishmash of jigsaw pieces that failed to make sense, more images tore through my mind, of Causia flying through trees, of multiple images of ogres attacking with demons. I was bewildered and tried to focus my mind to find the truth of it.

Flashes of movement ran across my eyes, some of our colleagues running, others of darkness and illusion. Here and there I caught glimpses of Pax appearing, then disappearing through trees. It was like a nightmare that I couldn't control. Just as I was about to give it up for a while, a voice, soft and tentative rang through my mind.

"Is that you Blender? I can sense your presence. You are nearby I think... But where?" I almost fell off the rock with surprise. Veritas approached, his arms full of firewood and asked if I was all right. But I waved him off so I could concentrate on the voice I was hearing. In my mind I heard my voice asking who it was, but I already knew. I'd recognise it anywhere.

"Stretch! How is it I'm hearing your voice?" My excitement grew as it was confirmed.

"Thank god you're safe. Is Brava safe? Are the others with you?" He sounded as though he was inside a tunnel or something, as his voice echoed as he spoke.

"Yes, we're all together on a high plateau above the Grunwald, trying to find you. We saw demons

103

everywhere... Where are you, and why didn't you tell me you were telepathic?" He laughed and it was a joy to hear.

"It never came up in conversation. But it is handy at times like these. I knew I could sense you nearby. Hope could too. I think you're not very far from where we're hiding. Stay where you are and one of us will come to fetch you. Give us about half an hour. See you soon my friend."

When I opened my eyes, I knew I probably had a stupid grin on my face, for all of my fellow travellers were now stood a few feet in front of me staring in amusement at me.

"You found them?" Brava asked, brows raised.

Patience handed me some food and drink, which I gladly accepted. "Yes, actually, they found me- they're all together apparently, somewhere nearby. Stretch told me somebody would come to get us in about half an hour. Great, isn't it?" I munched on my cheese roll ravenously.

"Of course, Stretch is telepathic." Patience said, smiling broadly.

"Did he sound okay? Nobody's hurt?" Veritas asked.

"I think they're fine. Stretch sounded okay and was all calmness itself. They must have found a good place to hide together. His voice echoed, like he was in a cave or tunnel when he spoke."

"Thank the gods for that. At last, something is on our side." Veritas said. They were reassured and Patience proceeded to help Arch feed and water the horses as we waited for someone to come.

As we waited, we heard far below us, beyond the sleet-heavy clouds, the constant screech and cackling of hordes of demons as they made their way through the forest towards Gardia castle. Now and then, we heard cartwheels, carving their way through the soft ground-carrying heavy weaponry perhaps. There must be hundreds, if not thousands of demons below. How are we to ever make it past them to save Axl?

A shuffling sound in the thick mist that had just collected around us alerted us to something close by and we all grabbed our weapons in silence. Brava and Arch were on their feet in an instant, their eyes scanning the swirling mist. Heavy breathing filled my ears. I stood up instantly, holding up my hand.

"Hold!" I said. "It's Stretch and Pax." I turned towards the approaching forms making their way towards me in the thick mist. "Over here." I called softly.

Pax's flushed face beamed at me suddenly as he stood inches away from my face. He clasped me by the shoulder and held my arm tightly in greeting. I noted several cuts and bruises to his face since we last saw each other. His hair was unkempt, as usual, like windswept snow, but it suited him that way, giving him the air of a natural hunter.

"Glad to find you alive my friend." he said as the others homed in on our voices. They lowered their weapons as they recognised him, and all welcomed both gladly. "And we're especially glad to find you still in one piece Brava.

Welcome back. Your skills are urgently needed if we are to regain Gardia,"said Stretch.

"What's the situation out there?" Brava asked, her eyes flickering wildly around for signs of others, but none appeared. We walked to the fire, where the horses rested, glad of the warmth.

We sat with Stretch and Pax to warm ourselves around the fire as Pax began to tell us their news.

"I'm afraid it's not good news. Gardia and the castle is completely overrun with demons, all led by Pinni. Some are guarding the Corridor of Sighs and the entrance to the Veil. It's impossible to get anywhere near our stronghold and the Wheel. Pinni has placed an enchantment on the Wall of Keys and the Cave of Artefacts, so none of us can fight against him. We have only the weapons Grinder managed to take from the Armoury before it went down. We barely escaped with our lives."

"What can you tell me of Axl?" Brava asked abruptly.

Stretch kicked the stones at his feet in frustration, his face clouded.

"She is alive- barely. Hope can sense she is still living, but in great pain. My mind is currently blocked to her. There was a lot of blood in the Guardians' Hall, and I think it belonged to Axl herself. I don't know what they've done to her, but it seems that whatever it is, has caused her to lose her powers." He stared at us all then continued. "I can't believe that Pinni has done this- but it seems he has been planning it for a while. I think it was he who arranged for you to be kidnapped Brava."

He saw the flash of her eyes as she took this in. "It does make sense now." She stared at us and swallowed deeply before continuing. "The last thing I can remember at Gardia was talking with Pinni and Shadow at lunch. I thought it odd at the time, that Shadow was more convivial than usual. He poured me some wine whilst we ate. All you others had finished and left for your quarters, but I had been delayed by a task Pinni had me carry out with Shadow. When it was done, Shadow and I had our lunch together and Pinni was the only person still eating in the dining room. He stayed to talk with us, but obviously they were both just drugging my food and drink as we talked. I was so stupid- too trusting." She huffed in annoyance with herself. "The next thing I knew was waking up inside that coffin."

"You couldn't have known their plan Brava. No one could have." Patience said. "Even Axl had no idea."

"I'm glad Blender found you and got you back." Stretch said. "The other Servants are safe inside a tunnel in this high crag. It's out of the wind and currently safe from the demons. I don't know what's happened to the castle staff or Novices. I pray they are safe somewhere. Will you all return with us? I'm afraid the horses won't be able to come though. It's a bit tight." He eyed the sleeping creatures.

"That's all right." Patience replied, standing up. "I will give them leave to return to their homes at their own leisure." She walked over to the creatures with Veritas and murmured into their ears softly as we prepared to leave once more. Veritas stroked True's mane as he bade him farewell. They both walked back to us, and Patience spoke. "They have decided to rest here a while, then they will return to their homes in Aerora. They were happy to help us and told us to summon them if we need their help in the future. They will be glad to help defeat the demon hordes."

"They said all that?" Grinder's eyes widened. Patience smiled. "Yes Grinder. They did."

"Okay, just checking. Shall we go then?" He pulled his cloak tighter about his head and grumbled to himself as he set forward behind Stretch. Veritas flashed his white teeth in a charming smile at everyone, in total contrast and Brava suppressed a small grin as she tightened her weapons belt once more.

We followed Stretch through the thick mist, taking one last look at the winged horses before losing sight of them to the elements. Their eyes had eerily held ours until we could see each other no more.

Our route took us through a narrow hole in the rock, to the side of the hooded outcrop, leading us into a slowly descending, winding tunnel.

Chapter 9

There was instant warmth inside the winding tunnel in the mountain. It was full of pockets of shelter from the cold wind outside, as the tunnel turned sharply in hairpin bends, seemingly hewn out of the rock by some ancient hands. Here and there, someone had created stanchions for torches, and some were lit as we passed along.

"Who uses these tunnels? It's not safe here if they are established routes." Arch said, his eyes scanning around the shadows as we descended further.

Stretch turned to face him briefly as he replied. "Don't worry, these are Causia's work. Nobody's ever been down here before. She just created them for us. To anyone else, they don't exist. The entrances are charmed, so no one but us will see them." I stared at him, not quite comprehending, but Patience seemed clearer on the matter and explained as we walked along together as Stretch led the way.

"You probably don't know, but Causia can create or destroy things if she sets her mind to something. She visualises what she needs or needs to destroy, and her magic conjures it. It's a safety mechanism if you like. She saw the need for a safe shelter and her mind came up with this."

I was still puzzled. "If she can make things happen, why doesn't she free Axl? Or imprison Pinni? " I asked.

Patience smiled but shook her head. "It doesn't work like that I'm afraid. Firstly, Pinni's magic is very powerful and secondly, she can't make something happen to another person. She can create things she needs with the environment around her- inanimate things, like shelters, caves, holes, walls- things like that. It's the best way I can describe it." I sort of understood and nodded. "I think I get it. A useful trick. Very helpful in our current situation."

"Yes. We will all need to use our skills to try and get our leader back where she belongs. Together, we must prevail, otherwise- it doesn't bear thinking about."

My brow cooled at the thought of a Gardia permanently filled with creatures of Chaos and Pinni in charge. I was glad of the distraction when flames from a fire danced on the walls at a curve ahead and voices filled the air. We had arrived.

"Brava! Thank the gods you are safely returned!" Causia stood, elated. Her long white hair and face was streaked with dirt and what looked like blood, as did many others in her midst. She embraced Brava warmly. I was taken aback as I had never seen her look this dishevelled, her trademark silvery white mane was usually perfectly tamed and streaked with one line of blue, but not today. Even her cobalt eyes looked wild.

"It's Blender we have to thank for that, not the gods." Brava replied, casting a warm glance towards me. I felt awkward suddenly, back amongst me peers and the old thoughts of being an outcast stirred in me. But Pax, as if sensing my dread, rushed to greet me, hugging me tight and made me feel better. It was good to have my friend back again. He smiled, his green eyes sparkling, clapping me on my shoulder, looking relieved to see me. His own white hair was still pristine, as if he'd newly spiked it this morning. I grinned; he always took pride in his appearance.

"It's good to have you back. I knew you would find her. Grinder and Hope told us of your great deeds. Well done." He pulled me to sit at the fire, where a bamchuck was being roasted on a spit. My stomach growled and saliva filled my mouth suddenly. I was very hungry,

"I wouldn't have succeeded without Arch and Patience's help," I said. "Together, we managed it."

I looked around at the faces. "What's wrong with Grace?" She lay to one side by the fire, her blue eyes looking unsettled. Pax answered.

"She'll be all right. I have been healing her wounds. She was speared by a demon as we fled, but it takes time for my healing to work. She'll be fine by morning, then we can move again. She was so busy creating an illusion to fool the hordes that a stray demon got to her from behind."

I looked to Arch, remembering suddenly. He realised it the same time and delved into his pack. He carried the vial over towards Grace and knelt beside her.

"Arch has Elinor's tears," I said. " A drop on her wound will heal it instantly." Pax and Veritas immediately brightened. It was far more effective than his salves and medicine. Patience helped remove Grace's dressing that Pax had placed there to heal the wound.

Veritas cradled Grace's head in his arms, her long, blonde hair cascading over her body. Arch undid the stopper and carefully placed a single drop onto Grace's wound. We held our breath as the jagged wound completely sealed up then disappeared entirely. It was truly miraculous. I had only heard of its power beforehand, never seen it in use. "I'm glad I thought to choose the vial." Arch said as he stoppered it and replaced it in its pack. I felt he was going to need it several times before this uprising was quashed.

Grace sat up; her blue eyes startled. Touching the location of the wound, she gasped to see it gone, then looked to us all and smiled. "Thank you, friends. I feel whole again." Veritas kissed her tenderly and she held him close.

We ate ravenously. It was a while since we had eaten real meat and the bamchuck was delicious. The Horn of

Plenty was useful of course, but nothing could replace freshly cooked food. As we drank to toast Brava's return and my efforts in procuring her back to the fold, I noted the signs of battle that these people sported on their faces and in their demeanour. Scratches and cuts were fading with Pax's administrations, but nothing could hide the weariness we all held with the turn of events.

"How did you all flee?" Brava asked. I too was curious to hear the answer. Hope responded first, her freckled face glowing in the firelight as its flickering light shone on the pale green tones of her hair. The very image of her radiated warmth amongst us as we sat around listening.

She always wore her clan's jewelled band on her forehead, and it mesmerised us as it reflected the fire's glow. Arch's arm draped over Patience's shoulder, showing how comfortable they were with each other. None of the others were surprised by this. I was obviously the last to know. It was a happy accident that I'd chosen them both for my quest.

"The first we knew that anything was amiss was when I stirred from my sleep on the second night since your departure. I woke from a deep sense of foreboding that was all encompassing, unlike a nightmare. I could see no detail, but I could smell blood and evil in the very air around me. So I got up and dressed. I intended to search the castle, fearing misdeeds." She shifted her weight and looked uncomfortable in the telling, but Brava placed her hand on hers in encouragement and she continued.

"As soon as I left my room alarm filled my senses, I could almost taste the blood in the air. I knew I needed to rouse the others, so I knocked on their doors, telling them of my fears. Only Shadow failed to answer. I didn't know then that he was part of the treachery." Her face hardened at thought of him, and Stretch muttered a curse.

"Stretch tried to communicate telepathically with Axl but drew a blank. It was like a wall guarding her mind. I could sense that Pinni was somehow involved but didn't know how. I urged Stretch not to communicate with him. Instead, we began to search through the castle in groups. Grinder teleported into Axl's room, but she was not there. He removed the Window on the World for safekeeping. What we saw on it was horrible- demons entering Gardia- everywhere. And Pinni at the heart of it all, commanding them."

"The bastard." Someone called out. Causia interjected. "We have it here- the Window on the World. It doesn't make for pleasant viewing."

Grinder continued the story. "I hid it initially, until I could figure out what was wrong. I teleported into the armoury and brought out all the weapons I could carry, to distribute them out amongst us. I tried to teleport to the Wall of Keys and the Cave of Artefacts but couldn't. Pinni had already cast a spell upon them, shutting us out."

Causia continued, her white hair draped like a cloak over her slender elven shoulders, "I flew over the castle to see if I could spot Axl, but instead, I saw it overrun with demons. They were scaling the walls to get in. I saw

Shadow in the courtyard, opening the gates wide open and more of them marched in, armed to the teeth. I knew we had to get out of there and quickly."

"When she told us," Stretch said, "we quickly gathered a few things and made to flee the castle with our weapons. But so many demons made it difficult, even with them. We fought our way through the corridors, killing demons where we could, and we got out onto the roof of the West Tower to look for a way to get to the forest. Causia was able to fly of course, and she could just about carry Grace, if need be, her being the smallest of the group. But we had to think how the rest of us could get ourselves out." She smiled at Grace as she continued.

"Grace used her skill to summon the winged horses for us all and we fought off the demons, as much as we could, until they arrived at the tower. Pax used his skill at hypnosis to enchant several demons that came too close as the horses arrived and Causia created a makeshift shield to cover us from arrows as we mounted the horses. It was only with our combined skills that we got out alive."

I sat there, picturing it all and I was glad that I hadn't been one of those Servants left behind having to deal with that situation. Although, I guess my own situation was probably close to it, in terms of demon encounters. So, where do we go from here?

The Window on the World told us very little of Axl's location, probably due to some magic of Pinni's no doubt. It was frustrating to think of his betrayal and all the opportunities we could have had in the past to destroy him. But then, we had no inclination of his treachery. Even Axl seemed unaware of it.

"So, do you think she's still in the castle somewhere?" Veritas asked as he rested his head on one arm alongside the fire. His beautiful face began to show signs of weariness too, with dark shadows creeping under his eyes. Grace's head rested across his chest as she lay with him, her blonde hair fanned out across his torso, catching the light from the fire. They made a pretty couple I thought. They suited each other.

"I can't think where else he would keep her." Pax answered. "Unless he has some hidden fortress somewhere we know nothing about."

"Can you see her at all Blender?" Patience asked, lying opposite me with Arch. I shook my head. "No, I've tried several times, but it's as though there's a black wall preventing me from seeing her. She's blocked from me, just like Brava was. Probably Pinni's doing."

"Gods preserve us! I hope she's not in a coffin like mine- I wouldn't wish that on anyone!" Brava said, digging her heel into the dirt floor. Huffs of annoyance followed. We were all tired and frustrated.

"So, do we risk trying to get back inside the castle to look for her?" Hope asked quietly. Nobody answered. We knew the odds of getting past all those demons in our way.

"Let's sleep on it, perhaps by morning we will have thought of a plan." Brava said, ending the conversation. As she lay herself down next to Stretch and myself, everyone settled themselves down for the night, safe in the knowledge that the tunnels were spelled against intruders.

For hours, my mind worked at trying to visualise Axl, trying to get some clues as to where she was, but in the end, exhaustion caught me, and I succumbed to sleep like the others.

 It felt different here, in the mountain. Different from the Wheel room. There, it was all business and professionalism. Everybody was guarded and afraid to displease our leaders. We were Servants of the Wheel and had great responsibilities laid on our shoulders to keep Gardia and the Outer World ticking over. It was up to us to set things right. But here, it was more now, we were friends, grouping together to try and solve a problem close to our hearts. For now, the Outer World would have to get by on its own.

But in saying that, we did take it in turns to keep an eye on the Window on the World all the same. It wouldn't do for that to fall into Chaos as well. For now, it was safe. But what would we do if elements needed our attention down there? Could we divide ourselves to carry out quests if the need arose? Could we afford to diminish our combined powers to serve both Axl and the World in our care? These things played heavily on all our minds. I could feel it and it didn't make for settled sleep.

My eyes opened upon a veil of silver white, like tendrils of spider casts, webbed before my face and I was momentarily disoriented. I rubbed my eyes to focus and pulled myself up from the floor, to see it was merely Causia's silvery white hair cast before me as she leaned down to add sticks to the fire. She had a pot on the boil for tea. The streak of blue that framed one side of her face glistened as the flames augmented.

She turned to me and smiled broadly, and it filled my heart with an unusual joy. "Good morning," she whispered. I sat upright and took in the scene. Several others still hadn't stirred from their sleep yet.

"What time is it?" I asked. "Oh, it's early yet," she replied, "I just wanted to get some water boiling to make us some tea with breakfast. You have a good half hour yet before daylight, but I couldn't sleep, so I thought I'd make myself useful."

Veritas sat up opposite me, looking only slightly better than last night. At least the dark shadows had disappeared from his eyes. Grace lay still asleep beside him, covered in his cloak. He passed me some bread and cheese, which I took gratefully. My stomach had woken before I had and was beginning to grumble. I swept my hair from my face.

"Thank you." I eyed the others as I ate and noted Brava's absence. "Where's Brava?" I asked.

Causia answered, "She went to look outside, to see if anything's changed below us. She won't be long." I relaxed again and began to think about how we were going to get into the castle to look for Axl.

The others stirred gradually and refreshed themselves in a spring Causia had created nearby. She thought of everything. I realised that we all needed to know what skills each possessed before deducing any methods of entry to the castle. There had to be a way we could pool together our talents to get a result, so I resolved to make that a priority after breakfast.

"Brava's returning." Patience said. I heard nothing, but minutes later, her tall muscular form appeared from around the bend and her face was grim.

"It's impossible. The whole forest is teeming with demons. They are camped all around us, probably all the way to the castle. I don't know how we'll get through them all." She sat down abruptly and grabbed some bread and cheese from the platter before us. Causia handed out tea to everyone.

I cleared my throat and took a gulp of tea before I spoke. "We need to know everyone's skills. Only then can we come up with a plan to get to the castle." I looked to them all, their faces now gazing upon me respectfully. Some nodded, Brava replied.

"That's a good starting point. Okay Blender, shall we make a list?" I nodded. Best to study it carefully if I was to come up with any plan. For some reason, they were looking to me to take charge. Perhaps it was because I had completed Axl's quest to find Brava.

So, Veritas wrote down the skills as each of us in turn told of our skills. As we made progress, I realised that I knew

119

very little of my colleagues' full list of talents. I knew of their main skills obviously, to select for quests, but the complete list was gold- precious and to be marvelled at. With this knowledge, we could do something, I was confident.

"And don't forget, we have the artefacts chosen by the three of us and my three keys." I added. Brava's face widened into a smile at last.

"Well done, Blender. I believe you might just have saved the day" she said, tapping me companionly on the shoulder.

Chapter 10

"What if Veritas transfigured us all into birds? Then we could fly into the castle avoiding the horde. Better than winged horses that can be seen by the demons." Grace said, her green eyes lit up with imagination.

"I'm sorry Grace, it's a great idea but it would mean sacrificing all our weapons and equipment. We would be without advantage, it wouldn't work. I can only transfigure ourselves without our weapons. " Veritas gave her an apologetic look.

"Oh, I see, I hadn't thought of that."

We thought some more, as we eyed up the list. "What if we did return to the castle on the winged horses, but I create an illusion so that we all just look like birds flying?" Grace asked again.

Brava's eyes fired up at the thought. "Yes, that might work surely?"

"Possibly," I said. "But there may be demons already at the towers waiting for us. Pinni has probably already thought about us using the horses to get there. We might be heading straight into an ambush."

Their faces fell again.

"A few of us could use the Shield of Darkness to get through the demons." Arch said. "But we need to get us all through." He looked despondent, which was unlike him. "If only there was an easy way to rid us of these demons." He stared at the list, willing something to jump out at him, but he was floundering, like the others.

"We need an army." Brava said. "We will have to find a way of amassing enough numbers to fight our way to the castle. The soldiers at Gardia can't all be loyal to Pinni-there must be many willing to fight for Axl's return. We've got to try and find them."

"But the same problem remains." Veritas said. "Getting through the hordes to find them. It's going to be the same difficulty for us. There's got to be another way."

"I can double our numbers, but even that's not enough to fight all those demons." Hope said.

"But it will be useful to double us up once we are inside the castle." Stretch said. "Twice as many of us to put up a fight at close quarters is a good idea." He nodded at Hope with a smile.

"And I can see through walls when we're there." Pax added. "Gives us the advantage."

"And if I see Axl, I can travel through walls to free her with Grinder," Pax said. The two smiled at seeing the possibilities arise. "But we still have the problem of getting past those hordes." Brava looked glumly at us.

Lots of little ideas popped up during the course of the conversation, but they were bitty- things to do once inside the castle. None offered a solution to getting through the hordes. Brava paced as she tried to think it through and we were all frustrated as several ideas came and went, dismissed as flawed in some way.

"I need some air." I said and got up to see what was happening outside.

"I'll come with you." Stretch stood up and walked with me. We grabbed our cloaks to protect us from the elements outside.

The closer we got to the tunnel's exit, the colder it became, and we tightened our hold on our hoods as we stepped out into daylight. The brightness was dazzling after being in the dimly lit tunnel. It had snowed heavily whilst we had been talking. That was bad news in itself, it meant we could not use the Shield of Darkness out here, our tracks would be seen in the snow, not to mention the lack of shadow until nightfall. Could we afford to wait until then?

Stretch and I sat on the sheltered rock on the plateau to think for a while. The horses had gone, and I couldn't blame them. The weather was bitterly cold.

The two of us watched the demon camps below in silence for a while and I became aware of the concentration upon

123

Stretch's features. I realised he was using his telepathic powers to try and gain knowledge from the demons below. After giving him some time, I asked, "Can you glean anything from reading their minds?"

He didn't reply at first, then turned to face me, nodding. "Bits of conversations. It's hard to isolate one voice from the crowds, but I did glean something useful. But you're not going to like it."

My jaw dropped as he told me what he'd heard. This was worse than we could imagine, and I wasn't sure we could do anything about it- not without Axl.

"Are you sure you heard correctly?" Brava's face visibly blanched. She kicked at the dirt in anger. "We can't let this happen! We must do something and soon."

"We know, but our only way of getting it done is by finding Axl. Only her powers will prevent the creatures of Chaos completely destroying the Outer World." Veritas said, his eyes glinting in the firelight. "It seems Pinni is intent on destruction now that he's in power."

Several paced the tunnel trying hard to come up with a solution, but the solution had been staring me in the face for a while. I turned to the others.

"I know what to do." My voice sounded stronger than I felt. They all turned to look at me, puzzlement written on their faces. Some had hope in their eyes. Their faith in me was touching. As they stood before me, I drew forth the Viridian key from my palm. "I will use this to get us there."

Hope's freckled face broke out in a smile and Causia rushed to hug me. I was taken aback, unused to such attention. "Of course!" she said. "I had half thought about making more tunnels, but it would take too long for me to fabricate them. But the key- it's just what we need."

"I'm not sure I understand." Pax said, as he eyed the key. I laid it out for him and anyone else that was unsure, what it meant. "The Viridian key allows us access underground, to wherever we need to go. It's like an instant tunnel creator. It will take us to where we want to go, underground, thus avoiding the demons."

"It can take us to the castle dungeons unseen." Veritas said with a smile. "Of course. Well done, Blender."

"Well, that's one part of the problem dealt with. Now we need to focus on a plan for when we get there." Brava replied.

We gathered around the fire to discuss tactics. I had a few ideas of my own, one of which was rather daring. I decided to hold back from suggesting it, leaving it as a last resort, if all else failed. For if I used the Ivory key, we could find ourselves in more trouble, as opposed to solving the problem of lack of numbers. There was no telling whether there was any loyalty to the Wheel still to be found amongst the Spirit World.

After an hour or so of putting together the semblance of a plan, we decided we were ready to set off to give it a go. We had a lot more to lose if we didn't try and time was running short.

I could foresee some trouble ahead, once we arrived within the castle, but I held onto my thoughts about using the Ivory Key for now, we might get lucky.

We gathered our packs and armed ourselves. Causia created more shields for us, as well as an ample supply of arrows for the fight ahead. Grinder had already supplied us with enough swords and spears from the armoury, so now we had a good range of things to help us tackle the demons once we got to the castle itself.

Arch doused the fire, the last job before we left. I took one last look at our refuge, then I glanced at everyone in their fighting gear, waiting ready to follow me to battle. It felt odd, to be relied on like this. This wasn't me. I was nobody's leader. Yet only I could wield the Viridian key, for it was still my quest- until Axl decided otherwise.

With one deep intake of breath, I grasped the key before me and led the way to the other end of Causia's tunnel, ready to invoke the power of the key, to send us forth to meet our fate. Meanwhile, the creatures of Chaos caused havoc down in the world of mankind.

I could see our position in my mind, as we carved our way through the underground towards the castle. It would take us a good part of the day, so we would arrive at the castle after dark. That was of some benefit to us at least. We had discussed coming into the castle from the dungeon and kitchen levels. Hopefully, they would not be occupied, giving us time to gather ourselves ready for attack.

After we came to the end of Causia's tunnel, the Key began to carve a new tunnel into the mountains before us. Holding the key ahead of me, the tunnel kept leading on, through bedrock, earth, and crystal alike. The tunnel wound its way for miles then abruptly, we fell forward into a cavern.

"What happened?" Hope asked, staring at the huge expanse before us. Patience held the Orb forward for us to see. And Hope doubled its lighting power so we could see further. It was huge.

"We've fallen upon a cavern," I said. "I didn't know it was here."

"How far are we from-" Arch was cut short as we all heard it, coming from ahead- demons!

"Get behind the Shield of Darkness." Arch said instead, holding it out in its full expanse before us all. We had to cower low, to avoid being seen beyond its perimeter. With our lights urgently distinguished, we hoped the shadow of the tunnel behind us would hide us well enough.

We froze where we were, behind the shield, as scores of demons, all heavily armed came scuttling through the cavern, their cackling echoing everywhere. I prayed we wouldn't be found. We weren't ready for this yet.

Among the demons were three cave trolls- ugly, malformed dumpy creatures with a profusion of hair on their bodies. They stood head and shoulders taller than the demons, so they were easy to spot. Unfortunately, I remembered suddenly that they had a keen sense of smell. And sure enough, just as the first troll came within spitting distance, it halted, sniffing the air, just yards from us.

I looked at my companions' faces and realised what was coming. I gritted my teeth and held tightly onto my sword. Brava was the first to lunge forward as the troll came directly towards us. Her war cry stunned the demons before us and as she dived feet first into the troll's torso, winding him, the rest of us charged forward, swords swinging, into the stunned pack of demons.

We hacked at the first few before they had time to react, but the next ones came running towards us, weapons raised, ready for a fight. I speared the next demon in the stomach and its guts spilled out before him as he dropped to his knees. My nose involuntarily wrinkled up in disgust as I carved my way through the next one in my path.

I was only vaguely aware of Stretch's form lunging past me and launching himself into another troll as he made the troll's weapons disappear, along with its hands, as Stretch sliced his sword through them. It floundered and Stretch stabbed him in the throat for good measure. He jumped clear just as the troll sank forward.

More weapons disappeared from our startled demons' hands, replaced by reeds as Veritas used his transfiguration magic upon them. Brava smiled and slew two demons with one broad swing with the side of her sword. Then she leapt onto a troll and pierced his skull with her jewelled dagger. He dropped like a stone.

Patience's heart arrows cut a swathe through several approaching demons, killing them where they stood. Stretch leapt forward with Arch, launching more attacks upon the oncoming demons. Several demon faces looked stunned by our abilities and some, I saw, decided to turn tail the other way.

"We must stop them getting to the castle!" Brava yelled, pointing towards them.

Causia spread her ebony wings and flew over the heads of the demons and launched her arrows into them further up the cavern. They had not banked on any of us being able to fly and they were caught unawares by her attack. Several fell as the arrows found their mark.

She had the presence of mind to create an illusion of a huge dragon, breathing fire, coming at them. They turned tail once again, returning towards us. Causia continued to fire her arrows at them with ease as she flew, as we fought the others before us.

Arch leapt fifty feet to fight by her side to help kill off the remaining rearguard. I had not seen him do a leap like that before. I knew he could but hadn't seen it. It certainly was impressive.

My own hands were slick with demon blood. It was oily and black and dripped down my sleeve, making the grip on my sword's hilt difficult. Veritas saw and threw me a pristine handkerchief from his jacket pocket to wipe my hands, before firing several more arrows into the demon crowd. Only he would have such a thing- and in newly laundered condition at that.

They were dropping like flies and several further up were on fire, after Arch had set his fire eyes upon them. They stupidly ran into each other, causing the others to catch fire too. Their screams were terrible.

Grinder confused everyone by teleporting to various spots amongst the demons and slaying them with his sword before they even realised, he was there. He was like a jack-in-the-box, popping up everywhere. I just hoped that Hope's fire spears didn't catch him unawares.

It was finally done. Dead demons and trolls lay knee deep on the cavern floor, bloodied or burnt, but vanquished. We drew breath once again and managed to smile at our victory. The first battle won. We had tested the waters and as a team, we seemed invincible.

Arch and Grinder between them got rid of all evidence of our passing here. Grinder made the bodies shrink to the size of toys and Arch used his fire to incinerate them into ashes. Causia used her skills to close the tunnel we'd come through and it was as if we'd never been here.

"You'd better wash their ashes into the ground Causia." I said, noting the grey pile left behind on the walkways. In seconds, all signs of the demons' existence had gone.

We felt slightly renewed by the sudden rush of adrenalin after fighting the demons and it felt good for something to go right at last. This skirmish proved that we fought well as a team, using our respective skills and weapons to full effect. It would not be long though until we would need to test them again.

We crossed the long cavern, making our way along makeshift rope bridges that someone had made. The whole time I'd been in Gardia, I had not known of these caverns. Who had created these bridges? They seemed well made, bridging the deep crevasse that held a fast-flowing river below us. I wonder where it led to, as did the others. Perhaps out to the sea? Maybe one day we would know.

Guided by Patience's Orb and some torches we found; we made our way along this new track to see where it led. Brava kept her keen eyes on the distance, being able to see as well in the dark as any night creature. Patience kept her senses alert for any further demon presence, her head constantly turning as if training her ears on any sound. Hope's diminutive body moved alongside her, her own head moving in tandem with Patience's.

"I hear something ahead, far away," Patience said, pausing. Hope's face turned to us too, her own senses stirring. "Yes, I sense more demons coming our way. But there's someone else with them. It's a familiar smell. But I can't quite place it."

"Gods- I hope it's not Pinni." Grace said, looking worriedly at Veritas. He held her hand in reassurance.

"No, it's not. He has an altogether different aura about him. There are several of them, whatever they are." Hope stood stock still, realising what she could sense.

"They're... Soldiers. Gardian soldiers." Hope's eyes widened considerably as I'm sure did mine. Brava's face lit up with hope. "They might help us.." She turned to me. "Blender- can you use your visionary powers to see if they are prisoners?" I nodded and closed my eyes in concentration.

Several fleeting images flashed by my eyes- of trolls and demons, of human battles against the hordes in the Outer World. Human blood was flowing through the streets, as they were massacred by creatures of Chaos. Pinni was at their lead, lancing his magic into defenceless settlements. It was terrible to see.

I recoiled and tried to concentrate on what was ahead. Then I saw it clearly. But it was not possible. I fell backward against the rocky wall, gripping it for balance.

"What is it, Blender? What do you see?" Brava's face looked at me intently and her hand clasped me tightly by the arm. I opened my eyes abruptly.

They all stared at me anxiously, but I had no good news for them.

"I saw them. Fifty or more demons and trolls together, but with them were an equal number of soldiers- Gardian soldiers."

"Are they in chains? Being held prisoner?" Veritas asked, eyeing me gravely. I swallowed hard. "No. They are marching alongside the demons, fully armed. They're all coming this way."

Chapter 11

"How long do we have?" Brava asked simply. " They'll be upon us in ten minutes," I said.

"Right, let's get organised. Pax, you position yourself further up inside the wall. Attack from behind once they've gone past you. Try hypnosis if you get a chance. Causia will support you from above. Choose somewhere high upon those rocks to wait unseen." Causia nodded and flew upwards as Pax chose his location carefully.

"I can teleport between them as before, to confuse them. And Veritas can make their weapons move out of their hands." Grinder said. Brava nodded.

"Hope, you've got your fire spears, if you position yourself over there, well-hidden on that high ledge, until the right moment when I instigate the attack." Brava said, pointing across to the opposite side of the cavern.

"Veritas, you and Pax will need to try and get inside the soldiers' minds. My feeling is that Pinni has enchanted them to be on his side, but if you counter that enchantment, we should get plenty of help from the soldiers. Veritas, place yourself high up next to Hope so you can get a clear view of them as they come."

Veritas smiled and set off with Hope. The two were used to working together on missions. He slung his bow over his shoulder to climb, pulling up Hope behind him into the shadows of the ledge.

"Blender, disguise yourself in the wall, close to where Pax is, you can be an extra weapon when Pax and Causia attack from the rear." I nodded and started walking towards Pax.

"Stretch, you, Grace, Arch, Patience and I will initially wait here behind Arch's Shield of Darkness. When they get close enough, I will lead the fight from the front while Pax, Causia and Blender bring up the rear."

"I can try and make a troll or two shrink too, if I try hard." Grinder grinned at us all.

"Hope, as soon as the action starts, double us all up, so we have twice the numbers on our side, then use your powers to attack the trolls, with what elements you choose. " She looked at us all in turn, satisfied that she had covered as much as she could in that short time. She smiled and nodded, held up her sword and said "For Gardia!"

We echoed her cry then prepared to position ourselves for the attack.

Very soon, the heavy footfall and cackling signified their
close proximity, and the rancid odour of rotting flesh and
filthy rags filled the air. I tried not to breathe it in as they
came closer. I sensed everyone else's distaste too, as I lay
in wait. Pax was only feet away from me inside the wall
and I could hear his heart beat faster as they approached. I
wondered if it felt the same for him, inside the wall, as it
did for me to blend with it. Perhaps not.

The soldiers walked amongst the demons; their faces
glazed in enchantment. We were right. This was Pinni's
doing. I was glad to see they were armed. If Veritas or
Pax can reverse Pinni's enchantment upon them, then we
will have a good chance of winning this attack.

There were far more demons than we had originally
thought, which was worrying. But I believed we could
win the day, with all our skills combined. We had to
prevail, or all Gardia would be lost.

The monstrous horde entered the cavern and my heart
pounded in my chest as the time closed in when Brava
would launch herself into battle. The demon bulk
entering past us was lessening and I prepared myself.
There it was! Her terrible war cry was enough to stun
anything in her path. The way she increased in size as the
adrenalin hit her body was a sight to behold. It would
worry anyone who came to fight her.

I felt Pax move nearby and I prepared to launch myself
forward, gripping the Sword of Justice with both hands.
As one, Pax and I hurled ourselves into the closest

demons at the tail end of the group, cutting through their limbs as they craned their heads forward to see what Brava was doing ahead of them. They were caught unawares and dropped like stones. But others around them, alerted to the danger behind, launched into a counterattack, turning back on us.

As Pax and I slashed and stabbed in an arc before us, Hope sent spears of fire into the heart of the crowd of demons ahead, setting them screaming, fully ablaze. They crashed into each other trying to rid themselves of the flames, but instead, caused others to catch fire as they touched them. Several dropped over the edge of the path at the narrow section, into the deep chasm that lay alongside, screaming to their deaths.

Pax and I saw several stunned faces among the demons, after they raised their weapons to attack. Their weapons suddenly crumbled to dust in their hands. It was Veritas, who had transfigured them, and I smiled. Their stupefied faces contorted further as Pax, and I slew them easily with our weapons.

I caught sight of Causia flying above, shooting poisoned arrows into several as she passed over our heads. I turned to look behind us, sensing more enchanted soldiers approaching, marching over the demon bodies we had slain. Pax was undoing the enchantment on them as quickly as he could, jumping to the ledge to avoid being struck. Arch moved closer to defend him, cutting a swathe through demons stupid enough to attempt a parry.

"What the?"- I was briefly startled by the sight of another me, fighting with a duplicate Sword of Justice five paces away. Equally, Pax looked twice as he saw himself further down the tunnel, cutting through three revolting looking demons. Hope had obviously doubled up everybody, but it was rather disconcerting to see it.

Brava's raucous battle cries pumped the adrenalin in our bodies, and we saw her and her double leap impossibly high over demons as they plunged their swords into demon skulls or shoulders from above. Both even ran over their shoulders and heads, digging blades into the demons as they carved their way through them.

Suddenly I heard several clashes of swords behind us, far more than should be from our small numbers. I was rapidly relieved to see that it was the soldiers, now fighting alongside us, to the horror of the demons accompanying them. Many demons were slain before they realised what was happening and I saw Pax's face grinning down upon them from the ledge next to Grace, as she cartwheeled along throwing daggers into the horde.

Veritas used his transfiguration skills to change a large proportion of enemy weapons into harmless dust or feathers and the trolls and demons who had been caught out unawares stared at them stupidly as they were attacked from all sides. When it was possible to retrieve it, I withdrew the Stone of Power from my palm and ran into the thickest part of action at the head of the crowd, ducking blows as best as I could. I felt a graze sting my shoulder as something hit me, but I carried on attacking the demons closest me as I ran. Once in place I invoked the Stone's power, aiming it at the remaining demons ahead. Like a wall of dominoes, they fell one by one until none were left at the far end of the cavern.

Arch helped Pax clear the way through the middle section of the horde as some of the soldiers tried to climb over the increasing mound of demon bodies. They made their way towards two large trolls pushing their way towards us from the rear. They still possessed their weapons, as Veritas hadn't got to everyone yet.

One of Grace's arrows sped across my line of vision suddenly, as she stood five paces away. It hit one of the trolls directly in the eye and it toppled over, crushing those demons closest to it. Another whizzed past seconds later, hitting an injured demon about to attack me with a hatchet. I nodded my thanks to her. At least I think it was her, it could have been her double.

I saw the two Causias flying around the cavern, one fired her arrow into a huge demon barging his way towards Pax, the other created a gigantic dragon at the rear, sending the scattering demons directly into the two Hopes' fire spears and to their deaths. A Heart arrow found its way into one of the demons too, as the initial arrow fired by Causia failed to kill it outright. It now dropped to its knees looking stunned, then died face down at Pax's feet. Pax's face was a picture of revulsion.

We had fought for near on an hour and we were making headway, despite the constant advance of more demons coming from the tunnel. But there were several mounds of dead demons blocking the path and it became hard to get over to the demons still coming at the rear. One of the Grinders saw the problem. He roared deeply as he held out his hands, finding a ledge to work from. As he cast his hands forward, the piles of dead demons were shrunk in size then pushed into the chasm, out of the way, leaving a space for us to continue the fight.

Brava led the charge again, launching herself into a high leap and landing with a scything motion across several demons with her sword. Her face was eager, her eyes lit up with fire. She was actually enjoying this battle. Her other self was similarly employed, leaping from ledge to path and slicing through the demon hordes as she progressed through their ranks. Despite seeing us do battle, the demons still kept on coming in through the cavern. How many more were there?

One Brava's face was bleeding from cuts gained in battle, as was one arm. The other Brava had no marks other than scratches to her leg. I wondered which was which.

I turned and narrowly avoided being speared by a large demon who still possessed his weapon, dodging just in time and I sliced his leg as I ducked. The Sword of Justice killed him instantly. I ran with a Pax and one Patience towards a large group coming over a stone bridge further behind, the scratched Brava with a Causia at the lead. One of the Hopes concentrated her spears of fire upon a second group coming behind them. They erupted in a ball of flame and dropped to the river at the bottom of the chasm below the bridge.

Patience fired several Heart bows into the leading demons, and they fell as we approached. Pax and I jumped onto their bodies and lunged downwards with our swords onto those beyond the fallen.

"Argh!" I cursed as something cut into my leg. Pax heard my cry and pulled me aside. While Patience and Causia attacked those nearby, Pax placed his hand on my leg to close the wound.

I felt intense warmth at his touch and the initial sting of the cut faded instantly. He withdrew his hand then touched another spot on my arm. I hadn't realised that I had been bleeding from another wound there too. In seconds, he had healed them both. I nodded my thanks,

We returned to the melee, launching ourselves upon the dwindling hordes, soldiers fighting at our sides, attacking fiercely to decimate the enemy ranks. Several felled two more trolls that were bringing up the rear and now, only demons remained. There were still some with their weapons, but others had been bewitched by Veritas' magic and were impotent. The fifty demons that remained were very soon dispatched, left to join their colleagues at the bottom of the chasm. Stretch's face smiled from across the chasm at me. We had triumphed and it felt wonderful.

Hope snapped her fingers as she jumped from the ledge nearby and all at once, our doubles disappeared. Only ourselves and the surviving soldiers remained to savour our victory. It had taken just an hour.

A lieutenant I recognised from Gardia walked over to us, amazement still lingering on his face. He bowed to us, his sword to his forehead as a sign of respect.

"What just happened?" He asked simply as he rose upright. Brava grinned broadly as she came to stand with us. I noted a few scratches on her legs, but otherwise she was unharmed. I smiled to myself.

"Lieutenant Frimm, glad to have you back on our side. I'm afraid it's rather a long story." Brava replied as she wiped her sword before sheathing it again. Grinder smiled at the lieutenant, which was unusual for him, and Frimm nodded politely.

We used the clear up time to recover our strength and to see to our wounded soldiers, whilst we planned our next steps in the tower. Pax and Patience were kept busy using their healing skills and the soldiers took a while to take in the severity of the task we had ahead. They had been enchanted maybe even before Brava went missing by what the lieutenant described as his last recollections of events.

At least Frimm recognised the passage we were in, it was a secret entrance into Gardia's towers from below ground. It wasn't used as a rule, only in times of battle, so it was no wonder we hadn't known of it. The last time Gardia was under attack was just before Axl was made Governor. It was lucky that Frimm knew of the route needed to get us to where we wanted to be. But before any demons came looking for those missing, Grace created an illusion that the cavern was blocked by rockfall at both entrances.

We were sure it wouldn't be long before some realised their troops were missing.

As we refreshed ourselves, Frimm drew a map for us in the dirt, of where it was likely Pinni would have posted his demons and guards.

"There will be many more soldiers under his enchantment up above ground." Frimm said grimly. "The men with me here are only a fraction of what Gardia possesses and there would be three times this number guarding the towers."

Veritas spoke up." The soldiers are no problem, just like with your men, Pax or I will take away the enchantment placed upon them, so they will add to our numbers instead. Also, I can transfigure the demons' weapons into useless items, so they'll be easier to kill."

"You can do all that?" Frimm's eyes bulged in surprise. Veritas nodded. "Then I think we will have a chance up there." The officer said.

"That leaves our greatest problem- Pinni himself," I said. "If he is up there, then he will not be so easily defeated. His magic and skills are powerful. I don't know if even all of us together can bring him down." They stared at me, knowing what I said was true. We might have won this battle, but this was just the tip of the iceberg. How were we to defeat him?

Brava stood on the rock ledge that crossed over the chasm, looking deep in thought. It was as though she was planning the attack in her head.

"Got any ideas?" Grinder called over to her. "We need to pool our thoughts together to plan this properly." For once, I agreed with him, and it went against the grain to do so.

We had never been friends and there was a long history between us, most of it with Grinder reinforcing Shadow's verbal attacks against me. He wasn't afraid of planting a few digs in my ribs when passing me in the corridors either. Between him and Shadow, they'd made life a real challenge up in the towers. Mostly I ignored it or kept out of their way. I didn't use my powers to retaliate, it never occurred to me to do so, even though I could easily hold my own.

Grinder's eyes caught mine looking at him and I wondered if he could read my mind. But he just moved over to make room for Brava on the ledge.

"I think we can make it into the towers easily enough," Brava stated boldly." but it's not that we must worry about- it's whether Pinni has enchanted the towers to refuse us access to the keep. If he holds Axl prisoner there, we will again need to combine our own magical skills to counter his- we must pool our resources to create the maximum impact, or we and Gardia are lost and that is unthinkable."

Chapter 12

It was easy to spot where the demons were clustered on our way up from the cavern into the tunnels leading up to Gardia's Towers. Their cackling told you where they were several minutes before you encountered them.

We waited for Veritas to transfigure into a bat to fly to where they were so he could see numbers and positions. We all had a plan and if we carried it out, we had a chance of getting to the tower. In a minute, Veritas returned and told us his findings.

"There's a cluster of them sitting around a stew pot twenty yards further up. There are only ten there, all busy stoking the fire and trying to chop things for the stew. They should be no problem. Further up the tunnel there's thirty or more just sitting there, resting up, waiting for something. They're in a more confined space than the others, so they'll be more of a problem to get our magic to affect them."

"Well, it's better than I thought," said Brava. "We'll deal with both groups as planned. Are you ready Patience?" She nodded and lifted her face upward and began to emit tiny little noises, cupping her hands to either side of her mouth.

It took only seconds for us to see the result of her actions and I involuntarily stepped back against the cavern wall at the sight- and I wasn't the only one, I noted. Grinder's eyes darted around to see if anyone had noticed him twitching with discomfort.

Hundreds of bats came swooping like a black cloud above Patience, their tiny wings creating a creepy sound as they listened to her voice. They seemed enchanted by her and gave the impression of listening intently. Then, with a wave of Patience's hand towards the demons, the cloud of bats swept along noisily towards the enemy, chirruping as they went. In less than a minute we heard the wails of the demons as they were attacked by the little creatures. Brava wasted no time and lunged forward, after her quarry, the rest of us following right behind her, armed to the teeth.

It was chaos ahead, as the demons flailed their arms about wildly, trying to stop the bats attacking their eyes and hair. It was our perfect opportunity to add our own attack to the mix, slicing with our swords as the demons were taken by surprise. Some died instantly before being able to even cry out an alarm and those left were quickly cut down soon after. Somehow, the stew pot remained upright despite the chaos all around it.

"Let's go!" Brava led the way again, as the bats already headed towards the demons further ahead, having achieved their goal here. We allowed a few seconds for the bats to cause trouble, then we launched into the demons once again. This time Arch heated the demos' weapons as he cut his way through the throng, making them drop them like hot potatoes, where the bats had not yet reached.

We used our skills wisely to help achieve our goal and although some demons escaped Arch's magic, Brava and Grinder cut through them in combination of teleporting and sheer skill in battle. In less than twenty minutes the demons had all been slain, so the next stage of our plan involved Grace's abilities.

The tunnel wound ever upward before we arrived at a fork. "Which way?" Brava asked Lieutenant Frimm.

"Both will get you to the Towers, the one on the left ends up in the food supply storerooms, under the Kitchen, the one on the right takes us to the courtyard and battlements. It's my guess that the demons will have gone to the right."

Brava's eyes were focused and menacing. I was glad she was an ally not a foe, no wonder Pinni wanted her out of the way.

"I think you may be right too, but nevertheless, I think we should split up so we can approach from both within and without. I will lead to the battlements; do I have volunteers for the route inside the castle towers?" She looked to us all.

"I will go through the interior, if Patience and Arch wish to continue with me?" I looked to them both.

"Of course." They both said and Pax quickly looked to Stretch, both nodded to each other, then Stretch spoke.

"Pax and I would like to go with you, my friend, if that's all right?" He said. I smiled, glad that Stretch and Pax still considered me their friend.

"I would be honoured to have you join us." I smiled. They nodded with a smile.

"Right then," said Brava, "we have our teams. Stretch, you can use your telepathy to keep our group informed of how far in your team are, so that we can support each other." Stretch nodded. She turned to Grinder and spoke, "Grinder can also use his teleportation to help you out should you need extra help at any time. It will be useful to find out where others are at any time." Grinder nodded too.

"Hope and Patience can use their senses to listen out for any sign of where Axl is if she is in the Keep anywhere. Stretch can let us know of any developments in that field." Finally, she turned to Grace to speak.

"Grace, you know what you have to do once we're up top? It will give Veritas time to do his transfiguration and Hope to double us up."

"Yes Brava, I'm ready. I think we're all ready for this." Grace said.

Lieutenant Frimm stood with his men; swords drawn in readiness. "And you can count on all of us for support." He said earnestly. So, each group set off along their chosen route, the bulk of the soldiers with Brava's team, but three soldiers from Frimm's army volunteered to support the kitchen group. It was meant well, and we took the offer gladly.

The tunnel to the kitchen narrowed gradually as we ascended and soon, we could only walk in twos, side by side without touching the walls. The sight of some wine barrels stacked in occasional niches on the right of the tunnel told us of how close we were to reaching the storeroom ahead.

There it was, the tunnel ended with an ancient and heavy wooden door with great iron hinges and brackets holding it together. No noise was discernible from the room beyond, and everyone looked to me for the next step.

"This is it- everyone ready?" I asked and all nodded with a sheer determination on their faces.

The door opened easily, the result of frequent dipping into the wine barrels down here I thought. The storeroom was devoid of people, and it was still and quiet in there, surreal, considering the scenes beyond the tower's walls.

I entered with Arch to make check it was safe, then we beckoned the others in. We slid along the many shadows created by the large casks and grain sacks in the dim candlelight. A mouse scampered silently along the wooden shelving that spanned one long wall and disappeared out of sight between two jars of preserves. I wondered just how much of my food had been contaminated by mouse droppings and I suddenly felt queasy.

"What is it?" Patience whispered beside me. I must have wrinkled up my nose in disgust.

"Oh, nothing, don't worry." I whispered back.

The stairs up to the kitchen was ahead of us and each tread sported a stoppered jar or urn upon the end. I don't know what they contained, I just hoped none would fall and break and make a noise as we climbed up.

"I'll go first," said Pax, "So I can see through the door before we open it." So, he wove his way between the sacks and jars and led the way up, being careful not to kick any jar over.

The wooden stairs creaked on the seventh tread and the rest of us by-passed it after Pax pointed it out. He stood at the top of the stair now and glanced back with a nod before disappearing into the very fabric of the door that led into the kitchen.

Stretch concentrated as Pax entered the door, listening out for Pax's thoughts on what he saw beyond.

"There are three cooks inside there, guarded by two Gardian guards at the outer door." Stretch whispered. "Two demons are standing over the cooks and making sure they're doing the right thing. One's got a long knife in his hands but the other one's just resting a hand on the pommel of his sword, grunting."

Pax eased himself out of the door. "Did you get all that Stretch?" He asked simply.

"Yes, it sounds easy enough." Stretch said. "Nothing you can't handle, eh?" He smiled at Pax and Pax's green eyes twinkled back a smile in response.

"Okay, as soon as I go through the closed door, I will hypnotise everyone in there temporarily before you all enter, and we can sort them out together. I'll tell you when it's safe for all of you to come in Stretch," Pax said. We nodded and Pax wasted no time re-entering the door once more, his ice white hair disappearing from sight in seconds. This time, Arch and Stretch waited at the door, holding the latch ready to charge in there when Pax was done.

Seconds later we were all piling into the kitchen to a scene that was hard not to laugh at. Demons, Cooks, and guards alike, all stood looking into space as though something really interesting was floating there. Arch wasted no time in killing the demons and Stretch used his telepathy to bring back the cooks and guards to our side. They woke, alarmed, and confused as to how we had all arrived in the kitchen. But with Patience's soothing words to calm them they soon came to their senses.

"Grand Servants- it's so good to see you back in Gardia." The chief cook bowed as he beamed at us all. "This has become a terrible place since the Guardian left. Do you know when she will be coming back?" His dark eyes looked to us hopefully, but his query answered our unspoken question. They didn't know what had happened to her.

"I was hoping you could tell us where she is Sir Caravel. We have come to find her- to rescue her." Arch said. The cooks' eyes crumpled at this revelation.

"You mean she is in danger?" asked Mistress Pargatti, the pastry cook, her pale grey eyes wildly looking for reassurance. The sous-chef, Mistress Miranda Shale wiped a tearful eye as they listened to this revelation.

"Yes, she is in great danger and Pinni is behind all this treachery, bringing Demons into the Towers. He has also enchanted the guards to do his bidding- but don't worry- Pax has disenchanted these you see before you." Arch replied.

"Do you know if Pinni is in the Keep?" I asked. The cooks hesitated and looked to each other and to the guards that had been with them. Sir Caravel replied. "He was here up until yesterday, for he had us prepare him a lavish meal in the Tower dining hall- him and his co-conspirators I am guessing they were. They had a cloaked guest with them, which we could not see his face, but Shadow was with him at the table too."

"But today?" I queried, pressing the point. One of the guards that Pax had disenchanted replied.

"He ordered a sturdy carriage and six horses this morning and left with the cloaked figure and Shadow in it. They headed North, I don't know where exactly. He has some demons and his troops with him."

"His troops?" asked Arch. "Do you mean enchanted soldiers?" The guard shook his head. "No, they are vile creatures from beyond the veil, bigger than a man and vicious. They hold no mercy towards anyone who gets in their way. We didn't travel with them- thankfully."

"Do you know who this cloaked figure is?" I asked. The soldiers looked agitated, eyeing each other anxiously before replying.

"I heard Pinni address him as Veiri, I think that was right?" The other soldier nodded. Arch's eyes lit up with fury and he stepped up to the soldier and I was sure he was going to kill him, but instead he took hold of his tunic and pulled his face up to his. His voice was barely audible, despite the silence in the room, like he was trying to restrain himself I thought. One of his hands was perilously heating up.

"You are sure he called him Veiri?" The man nodded furiously, unable to reply with fear. He stared at him a few seconds before releasing his grip on the petrified soldier, then he whirled to face us, his face ashen.

"There's only one creature with that name- Veiri Dur- Ruler of Chaos." He spat the words out as though his very name caused him revulsion.

All our eyes were wildly trying to make sense of it. Why would Pinni have dealings with this creature- the one thing that Gardia sought to keep in the Underworld where he could not escape. His very presence here meant that creatures of evil everywhere were now able to infiltrate the Outer World- and Gardia itself so it would seem. Not one of us could counter that, not without Axl's powers. Even Pinni couldn't possibly hope to deal with such an unpredictable creature without fear of Death for himself. Why would he risk it?

Chapter 13

We all knew of Veri Dur from all our teachings as child apprentices to the Wheel, but he was contained in a part of our minds that kept knowledge of evil things under control, where they could not cause us nightmares. Stories we'd been taught about him were graphic and full of torment and without the administrative care of our Guardian teachers we would not likely remain sane from the nightmares they could give us after hearing of his deeds. Now he was here, and all those thoughts returned.

"You know who he is then?" Sir Caravel asked. " I see by your reactions that he is one to be feared. How is it that someone like that comes to Gardia to roam free?"

"How indeed." Stretch replied caustically.

"We must move on if we're to find Axl." I said, breaking the tension in the room. "Even though I don't sense her presence here, we still need to search the Keep and the

Towers." Arch's hand cooled again, and his face returned to focus. "Are any demons beyond the door?" I asked.

"No, I don't think they are this low down in the castle. They tend to move around the battlements and the towers." The soldier replied.

We gave our thanks and left the three guards to watch over the cooks to keep them safe, whilst we crept out of the kitchen into the hallway beyond.

The long corridor held more rooms to the right, but to the left, at twenty-yard intervals, were stairs that led up to the towers and the battlements. The long hall beyond looked to be empty.

"Let's show Brava where we are," Arch said, leading up the nearest stairs up to the ramparts. We followed quickly, eyeing the shadows as we went. The noise of battle struck our ears as we closed in on the door that led onto the bastion on the second-floor level. A blaze of daylight initially stung our eyes as we opened the wooden door out onto the stone battlements beyond. It had been a long while since we saw daylight.

We immediately engaged into battle as several demons came running towards us, weapons aloft- hideous creatures of the underground with misshapen forms and putrid flesh. My sword found purchase in several as I ran into the thick of it alongside Arch and Stretch. Stretch's eyes emitted their beams of searing fire, cutting into the flesh of those coming our way.

From down below, where crowds of demons and soldiers alike battled it out in the long courtyard, Brava's voice and large form was unmistakeable as she called to us gleefully. "Glad you could make it! Better late than never... Die you evil filth!" She added as a creature tried to lunge at her, lopping off his head in one swift movement. We grinned and continued with our own battle where we were.

Several more demons came running from all directions towards us and immediately our numbers were doubled up as Hope used her magic to create our clones. They scythed through the rushing crowd like a knife through paper, the demons dropping in their dozens before them. Several black arrows filled the air as Causia flew over the ramparts across the courtyard, spearing the enemy with their poisonous tips. Patience's Heart arrows soon joined them, diminishing the enemy even further.

More creatures came rushing down from the towers, crashing through the tower doorways that we'd just come through. "Looks like the whole of Pinni's friendship circle are here." Pax jibed whilst causing damage to the oncoming horde with his sword and axe. It was becoming a veritable bloodbath everywhere.

Arch's sword of Glass was effective in destroying these demons too. Just a touch of the sword killed them outright.

Grace leapt effortlessly from the courtyard onto the nearest rampart and started waving her hands before her, deep in concentration, whilst Veritas protected her back.

Suddenly a huge multi-headed venomous serpent, each head the size of a man, appeared in one corner of the courtyard. Its heads started hissing and ejecting spiked tongues towards the demons before it, as it slowly slid along.

The demons turned and fled, trying to exit the courtyard any way they could. But the Servants were already in place at the exits, ready to deliver those in blind panic to their deaths. In their keen interest to flee from the monster, they had not realised it was just an illusion that Hope had created, and it was working a treat to round up the surviving demons.

We could see that Pax's hypnosis had affected those soldiers of Gardia that were in the battle, reversing the spell that Pinni had placed upon them. All were fighting on our side as soon as Pax had arrived on the scene.

The battlements were almost devoid of demons now and Grinder appeared before me, having teleported from below.

"Can you sense Axl anywhere nearby?" He asked me, his arms and shoulders caked in black demon blood.

"No, not since we returned to the castle. Have you teleported to all the rooms and towers yet?" I asked.

"Not all of them, shall we go look together? We'll take Pax in case we encounter problems." I was unused to this version of Grinder, and I still found it hard to trust him fully, but I nodded. We told Arch we were going before we left. He could easily cope without us, I was sure.

We covered familiar ground, but it all felt different-violated and tainted. The Wheel Room doors were wide open but there was no one inside. I walked up to Axl's seat and touched it, hoping for some useful images that would help our search. Nothing.

"Anything?" Pax asked. I shook my head. My eyes hovered over Pinni's seat, wondering if I could bear to touch it, in the end, I did. Images of deception and treachery rushed through my mind like a torrent, overwhelming me with emotion. In every vision I saw Pinni plotting and destroying or using magic to murder or maim. It was too sickening to bear. I saw no images that would lead us to Axl. I pulled away.

"Nothing let's search every room," I said.

We moved on without encountering any more demons and our route through the Keep and the Towers went smoothly. We even managed to get into Axl's room, with its empty space on the wall, where the Window on the World had hung. I closed my eyes to concentrate on every item of furniture in there, touching some, where the images were strongest.

Below the chair where Axl would sit to read, there was a large blood stain on the carpet. In places it was still damp. I braced myself and touched it.

"What is it? What do you see?" Pax's words brought me to my senses again and when I opened my eyes, I saw that I had knocked over the chair and kicked the carpet in alarm as I fell backwards on my butt on the floor. So vile were the images I had just seen in my mind.

"He cut her arms off- in here- without mercy." I stuttered, my stomach churning at the still vivid imagery. "She was conscious the whole time but never cried in pain." I ran to the window and threw up. "How could Pinni be so evil? All this time he had fooled everyone."

Pax's face was almost as white as his hair and a tear dropped from his green eyes onto his tunic. It was the first time I'd seen him cry; I think.

Grinder paced the room, muttering to himself, fuming. Eventually he said, "I'll be back in a moment." With that he disappeared.

Voices from the corridor outside stirred me from my misery. "It's Brava and the others-" Pax went to the doorway and stuck his head out. "In here."

"What's happened?" Brava's face was full of concern and the others came to the room to join us. I told them all that I had seen, and they reacted similarly. Hope alone seemed to be coping. She came up to me and held my arm gently.

"I sense she is still alive Blender," she said. "And if she is still alive... Pax can heal her- can't you Pax?" She looked from me to him, willing it to be true. I nodded but kept to myself the thought that although we could possibly restore her limbs, we would probably not be able to restore her powers.

Grinder popped in front of us just as we were wondering what to do next.

"I've been to every room in the Towers and upper Keep, there's no sign of Axl or even evidence of her passing. But I did manage to shrink down and kill the demons guarding the Cavern where the Wall of Keys are kept. I think we should go down there. How safe is it up here?"

Brava replied, "All the demons inside the battlements and Towers are dead and Causia and Hope have used their powers to rid us of the bodies. All the guards are back on our side now and have been placed on guard duty throughout the Castle. Hope has doubled their numbers as an extra precaution. Around nine hundred previously remained within these walls. We've enchanted the entrances to prevent more demons coming in too."

"Good, so we can use our time to see what's happening down there before deciding what to do then." Patience said. She was right of course. We had to do something- but what? Where would we start looking for Axl and would bringing her back even bring an end to Pinni's plans? I greatly doubted it.

Periodically, I touched the walls of the Keep as we descended to the caverns where the Wall of Keys were kept. I saw flashes of activity, mainly Pinni and his troops passing through, but no sign of Axl. Nothing useful.

"Well, we're here, only you can go through to the Keys." Brava said to the three of us. "I don't know if you will be able to change any of your keys- should you need to, but we are on a quest all the same, only a different one now. Be careful what you do Blender." She nodded to Arch,

Patience and me and stepped aside to let us continue into the cavern.

"It all looks the same." Patience observed as we stood facing the Wall of Keys.

"There might still be an enchantment upon it though, so be careful Blender." Arch said. I nodded, my stomach fluttering, anxious to get this done. I sat on the floor and crossed my legs before the Wall.

"What's he doing?" I heard Patience whisper. Arch did not reply, probably because he didn't have a clue either.

I closed my eyes and placed my hands palm down to each side of me on the stone floor and in an instant, there it was... A clear image, as though Pinni himself was right here, before me, and I caught my breath in surprise, wondering if he knew I was here, but he didn't turn around.

I listened, concentrating on his every move and every sound as his fingers twisted and waved before the Wall. I recognised the warding spell as the Wall glowed and sparkled with energy. It settled again as Pinni's hands fell to his side- but he wasn't finished. I watched in awe, as he cast a spell upon the very ground before me, at the foot of the Wall Beyond my feet. Even though this was only an image of things Past, I could feel the ground beneath me tremble from his power. My hands pressed harder onto the floor to keep a grip on the scene, and I was glad to have continued, for it gave me a clear glimpse of Veiri Dur, who stood to the right of Pinni as both moved away.

My eyes snapped open, and I took a deep breath after holding mine so long. Behind me, Patience gasped and stepped towards me.

"No!" I called out urgently. "Stay behind me, the floor and Wall before me are enchanted." I got up carefully.

Arch and Patience looked at me worriedly and I ventured a small smile of reassurance.

"Did you see him?" Arch asked simply. I nodded.

"I saw it all. Pinni was here with Veiri Dur-" Patience gasped again. "Oh, how could he bring such an evil creature to one of our sacred places?" She shuddered as she envisioned it.

"Did you see what Pinni did?" Arch asked. "Can you counter it?" I nodded again.

"He has double hexed the area, but I saw how and I think I can undo it. I've got to give it a try." I said, hoping this was true.

"Is there anything we can do to help?" Patience asked.

"No, I don't think so- but wait- yes. Arch, I will need you to hide me with your Shield of Darkness whilst I invoke the counter hexes. That way, Pinni won't see me change anything- I hope."

"Good idea. I hope it works." Arch unhooked the Shield and as I went to stand before the enchanted area, he placed the Shield over me so I was encased in darkness. Both he and Patience stepped further back to give me enough space to work. I was alone in the dark once more, a place I was used to, but this time, people counted on me.

I stared ahead at the floor before me and extended my hands outward concentrating on evoking the Stone of Power from my hand. It came easily and glowed with purpose as I began my incantations. I held it tight as I said the words and swept my hands before me, covering the air above the floor before my feet and beyond, to the Wall itself.

A roar filled my ears as the cavern floor started to rumble with the effects of the Stone's power. Dust and grit and small stones elevated from the floor and remained suspended in the air a foot from the ground, quivering as though shaken by some force. I swept my hands sideways from left to right, then up and down, and with the downward movement, the grit, dust, and stones fell to the ground once more. I picked up a stone at my feet and tossed it before me. Nothing.

"The floor's safe at least," I said softly. "Now for the Wall of Keys itself." Patience and Arch stayed still where they were, and I could sense their relief without looking at them.

Again, I raised my hands, the Stone ensconced in my palm. One by one my fingers on my left hand moved up and down as I twisted my hand this way and that, my mind concentrating on the Keys. I closed them again and did the same with my right hand, the Stone now transferred into my left palm. I felt the very air around me suck my breath away and I had to gasp for breath several times as I twisted my hand in the prescribed shapes before me. Gradually, the air relented and I could breathe again normally as my hand completed the counter hex. Had I done it?

I de-activated the Shield of Darkness and turned to face my colleagues. "It's done. Now to test it," I said.

They smiled broadly and stepped forward to congratulate me, Patience with a hug and Arch with a firm pat on the shoulder. "I knew you could do it Blender." Patience said. "We both did."

I managed a smile and prayed what I'd done was sufficient. "Right here goes," I said, turning once more to face the Wall of Keys.

The Keys in my hand suddenly detached themselves from my palm without invocation and I knew then that what I had done had worked. They drifted through the air back into their niches. Now the Keys all glowed their bright colours on the Wall once more. Each in its niche, waiting to be selected.

I hoped that they would allow me to choose again without Axl, if not, I would lose huge advantages in our quest to find her. Maybe we would even fail without them and that was unthinkable. I had thought hard about the Keys and about any changes I would make, and I knew that I would only change one

Chapter 14

"You changed it? But you can't be serious- you really think we could go there and come out alive?" Brava's face was incredulous, her brows creased with worry.

"I felt I needed it," I said, trying to calm her. "There was something tugging me towards it... It could be Axl." Brava whirled to face us, looking from face to face, in question. Arch spoke up for me.

"You know how he senses things. He has visions of Past, Present and Future events. This must be something calling him Brava. We've got to trust his judgements- after all, he found you despite all the odds against it."

Brava's hands rested on her waist, she took deep breaths and nodded, her size decreasing back to normal again. I wondered how she had controlled it in that coffin, but I didn't dwell on it.

"Okay, so we have the Ebony, Ivory and the Viridian, what do you propose we do next?" Her eyes focused on mine, and I remembered she was on my side.

"I am going to change one of my artefacts as well, so any spells on the Cave will need to be dealt with first," I said.

"Really?" Brava asked. "Which artefact are you changing?"

"The Sword of Justice," I replied, to which all three gasped in unison. "It's all right, I've thought about it. We'll keep Arch and Patience's artefacts as they are, I think they'll still be useful."

"So, what are you going to choose instead, may I ask?" Brava said rather sceptically. "I will choose the Wand of Destruction."

Well, that shut them up and without wasting any more time I led the way into the Cave of Artefacts. I stopped abruptly as I came to the waterfall, sensing something wrong. I held my hand up to halt the others. They stopped without saying a word. I picked up a fragment of stone beside my foot and threw it onto the path ahead, beside the waterfall.

Immediately the waterfall expanded dramatically, increasing tenfold to flood the entire path and river beyond. Anyone who would have been caught on that path would have drowned in the torrent it created. A huge whirlpool appeared in the river that filled the chasm alongside us and it sucked up the waters with great power, like a thirsty giant, taking in the waters until the torrent had returned to a trickling stream.

We stared in horror, thinking what would have happened to us if we hadn't stopped where we were.

"He's used the expansion spell," said Arch. "I can deal with this if you like?" He looked at me, hopeful of being useful. I smiled and nodded, glad to let someone else do the hard yards. Patience and I watched as Arch countered the spell and soon, we were passing the waterfall safely. The Cave of Artefacts looked as it did when we were here last, and I could not sense any enchantments.

"So, this is the famous Wand of Destruction," said Patience, eyeing up the gnarled dark wood as I held it in my hand. The Sword of Justice had been laid reverently back where I got it from. It had done me a good service and I thanked it for doing so. "It's not very big, is it? I expected at least twelve inches." she said. I laughed.

"I should have thought that of all the Servants you would have known that size does not matter Patience." I grinned and she blushed, taking a different meaning to mine obviously. With Arch's look of concern, I decided to quickly add, "After all, look at me. I'm short, but I pack a good punch when I need to." She relaxed and smiled more easily, as did Arch. Foot. In. Mouth.

"But why not keep the Sword of Justice? Surely it kills as much as the Wand does?" Patience asked again.

I looked at her, conscious of what I said, so I wouldn't cause her embarrassment again. "You're right, but I realised there is no justice in Chaos, none at all.

167

Everything there is rotten and twisted and the Sword would not wield Justice should we find ourselves there. No justice can be wrought from those evil beings. Death alone isn't enough, the creatures of the Underworld would prevail even after death, as you know, so only destruction is enough to rid us of those monsters. For that, I need the Wand of Destruction."

Patience and Arch both looked at me as though seeing me for the first time, as though marvelling at seeing something new. They nodded and looked from me to each other before Arch said, "I could never have thought of that in a million years."

Patience interjected. "Me neither, you truly are a great Servant Blender. You've hidden your talents too long." Now it was my turn to blush.

In the Wheel room we all sat at the table to discuss where we go from here, as usual we expected Brava to take the lead, but I was wrong. All eyes looked to me expectantly.

This was new and unexpected, and it felt strange to be the speaker rather than the listener. I took a deep breath and opened my mouth- and froze for a second, but Causia caught my eye and smiled encouragingly, and I straightened. I couldn't mess this up, not now.

"Well, I think it would be sensible for some of us to stay here to help the guards protect Gardia. We don't want the Castle and the Keep falling foul of demons again, let alone allow Pinni to return here."

Grinder made a comment under his breath. I looked at him directly, as did some of the others and I said, "What

168

did you say Grinder? You have a comment?" I gave him my best challenging face.

His face crumbled. He wasn't expecting this, but he recovered and said in a more subdued tone than he usually used with me, "I simply said that it would be impossible. No one here can stop Pinni. We're not powerful enough."

I kept an even gaze and responded calmly. "That's where you are wrong. I alone countered Pinni's enchantments in the Wall of Keys and the Cavern of Artefacts. If I can do it, anyone can. But more to the point, I'm not expecting anyone to stop Pinni on their own. You have seen for yourself how we work well as a team- together we are more powerful. We can do it; you've just got to believe in yourself."

A spontaneous applause followed from the others; some even rose to their feet. "Well said Blender, well said." Brava stood clapping loudest. Grinder looked crestfallen and was reddening, but he did not give any bother after that. So, I laid down my plans for the mission, most of which everyone thought was advisable, if we were to keep Gardia safe. Some details, however, took them by surprise and a few questions were asked, to justify my choice of actions, but my answers satisfied them, for now.

"It's a good idea," Grace said. "That way, all of us get to go and find Axl and all of us are here to protect the Castle as well. Hope can easily double us up like she did before, and our clones will make the same decisions as we ourselves would make."

"I still think we should take some soldiers with us as back-up," said Grinder. But it was Stretch that saved me from replying.

"Haven't you listened to anything Blender has said? We don't need soldiers, together, we are more than capable of bringing Axl home, you just have to believe it." This was the first time I'd seen Stretch look annoyed, and I was impressed how scary he looked with his eyes powering up automatically with the adrenalin build up. I half expected to see them emit their beams onto Grinder, but they didn't, thankfully.

"So, we can take weapons we need from the Armoury, but unless we were elected to undertake a quest, none of us others can take anything from the Cave of Artefacts to help us?" Hope asked.

"That's right, so choose wisely what you think you might need," I replied. "When do we go?" Grinder asked.

"As soon as you've got your weapon, we're gone," I said. Several raised eyebrows popped up, followed by everyone getting off their chairs ready to fetch them. They paused as I added, "We'll leave the Window on the World where it belongs and that way, both Stretches can communicate any new developments in Gardia or the Outer World." They nodded and left for the armoury, their faces showing their eagerness to get started.

Causia came over to me. "Do you know where you are going to start looking?" She asked.

I paused briefly before replying, to make sure there were no new developments in my head since last I looked.

"Yeah, I think so- unless anything changes in the next few minutes." I replied cryptically and she grinned broadly and with a peck on my cheek she headed off towards the Armoury.

My face grew incredibly hot as I felt myself blush and I quickly took in some deep breaths to relax before getting my own gear in order. In ten minutes, all of us stood ready at the portal, waiting for me to choose our path in the Corridor of Sighs.

My fingers touched the web thin veil of mists, feeling for any indication of where we should look. I jerked in pain and pulled back as the others looked on worriedly.

"What is it, Blender?" Causia asked, rushing to my side. I opened my eyes again and glanced at my fingers, expecting to see blood, but there was nothing there. I looked up at the faces around me, all full of concern.

"Has Pinni jinxed the portal?" Arch asked. I shook my head. "No, it's not that- I felt her pain. She is badly hurt and has passed through here in chains. They have beaten and maimed her... It was horrible."

A lot of hissing and cursing around me confirmed their disgust and sadness about Axl's treatment. Grinder spoke first. "But did you see which way we need to go- assuming she's still alive?" I nodded. "Yes, she still lives, just. I saw the way. Follow me, keep your weapons at the ready."

My eyes and ears and even my sense of smell guided me forward through the veil into the Corridor of Sighs, my colleagues following tightly behind with weapons drawn.

171

The screeches and screams that echoed in my ears were painful and I thought for sure that everyone else could hear them too. "Can you hear them?" I asked, glancing behind me. Most shook their heads.

"I can," Hope and Patience replied in unison, their faces grimacing. "It's the demons, isn't it?" Hope asked.

"Yes, I think so. I guess we follow their noise."

I pulled away at a point in the sensory filled corridor where the pain was severe and held forth the ebony stone. We immediately fell into a twisting spiral of air that was filled with monstrous creatures trying to spear us.

I lunged with my wand at any evil attacking in my direction and each demon caught in its power faded into dust to join the spiralling tornado, for this was what we now found ourselves inside. From all angles within the spiralling winds, opportunistic creatures tried to slash at us or spear us with their weapons, but luckily, we were all prepared with our weapons and armour and kept up a force to contend with.

We were caught in this seemingly never-ending tornado and as we spun through it, I wondered if it would come to an end. We were constantly fighting off the hordes as we fell and soon, I feared we would run out of energy.

"Hope- can you do something to control this?" I called over to her as she speared a Slime-Wort. She nodded and Brava and Arch surrounded her as she wielded her powers to control the tornado that was holding us in its grip. It was no doubt, a Pinni induced trap.

As we continued to fight off the demons, gradually
Hope's powers over the elements diminished the force of
the tornado, in the end causing it to lose its power
entirely. As the demons dropped to their deaths,
thousands of feet to the craggy ground below us, Causia
whipped a carpet beneath us and gave it the power to fly
us safely to the ground. She smiled at me as she flew
alongside the carpet, making sure we were all safe.

"I think you have an admirer there buddy." Pax whispered
in my ear. So, it was true then. I wasn't imagining it. She
likes me. My body felt warm, and I felt a happiness I
hadn't felt before. This was new and I hoped it was going
to last, if only a little bit longer.

We touched down gently upon a land seared by war and
fire. Even the rocky ground had sooty residue upon it and
I wondered where we were, for none of us recognised it.

"Where's the sky?" Grace asked, looking up into complete
blackness. No stars, no clouds, no moons, or suns to
guide us, but the ground itself gave off a small amount of
luminescence which staved off the pitch black, enough
for us to see around us.

As Pax and Patience healed wounds inflicted by the
battling demons, I crouched to touch the nearest large
rock to see which way to go. I shuddered at its touch,
feeling the grimness all around me. "This is not a place
any of us wants to be," I said, swallowing hard. "It is
filled with your worst nightmares, and it will fight you in

173

mind as well as in body. We all need to watch out for each other down here."

"Where are we?" Pax asked as he stared at the grim reality around us.

"It is a land where nothing lives, a land where no one escapes from. Some call it Sheol or Gehenna, the Netherworld, where there is burning and separation. Most people know it as Hell."

Chapter 15

All around us, the very ground seemed to cry in pain, its luminescence disconcerting and we stopped to listen for a few minutes before moving.

"What do you think is making all those sounds?" Brava asked, her voice barely a whisper. It was unusual for her to be spooked, she was the bravest of us all, but here she was, unsteady on her feet and eyes darting about.

"I don't know for once." Veritas said, looking equally suspicious of every variation in sound.

I crouched down to feel the fragile fragments that were spread on the ground everywhere, giving off this eerie pale green glow. It reminded me of poisonous gas that soldiers used to use on their enemies to kill large numbers together.

"Be careful Blender..." Causia called softly. But I knew it was not harmful.

"It's okay, it won't harm us." I said, as my hand reached out to touch the tiny fragments. A shiver ran through my whole body as soon as my fingers touched the ground. I shot back upright and wiped my hand against my leg to wipe away the discomfort.

"What did you see?" Patience asked, her face locking with mine urgently.

"It's not what I saw, more what I felt." I replied. "The ground is littered with the dead- these are fragments of their bones, as they died here after a near eternity of torture and pain. The luminescence is their remaining essence, or spirit, if you like."

Grinder spread out his arms to balance as he lifted his feet up one by one, grimacing with revulsion. "Ugh, dead people? We're walking on their bodies?"

"Not their bodies- their bones." Veritas confirmed, his beautiful face tinged with sadness. He touched his forehead with his fingertips and whispered a prayer.

The carpet of crushed bones spread as far as the eye could see in this dim light and we could not avoid stepping on them. Only Causia had the luxury of flying off the ground instead.

I was drawn towards spiked peaks that loomed from distant shadows in the grey and I led our band forward, grimacing with each footstep as the bones crunched beneath my feet. My companions remained in a close group around me, eyes ever wary and ears listening for anything of note. But only a constant groan and whimpering filled the stale air around us.

We stared as the peaks loomed before us. They were impossibly high, even craning our necks to peer, we could not find their end, for they were swallowed into the darkness. As I headed for the all-absorbing darkness ahead of me, I called to Patience to bring the Orb forward.

"What is that?" Arch was trying to make out the shape beyond our light. "It's like a void. There's no light penetrating it."

It was true, even as we neared this apparent crack in the spiky mountain before us, the Orb's light did not reveal its form or reflect anything within. It was as if it absorbed every light and distinguished it. Worst of all, I knew that we had to go through it.

We stood a few feet away from the blackness before us. The crack was no more than ten feet wide and as tall as a Stone Giant, big enough for a cart and demons to enter. But the total darkness was disturbing.

"Shine the Orb in the opening Patience." I said and she walked forward with its beam circling her with its powerful light. But the moment it hit the entrance to the crack in the rock, it diminished into a candle's glow.

"Its light doesn't work in there!" She gasped with worry.

They all looked to me, and I felt the pressure of this new role I had been given. I was no leader, but yet- I had been chosen to lead this quest. Could I do it? I closed my eyes and concentrated my mind and a flash of light struck me

177

instantly. I opened my eyes and found all faces staring at me anxiously.

"I think I know what to do," I said. I walked back a few paces and withdrew the Ivory key, holding it in my hand, pointing it towards the ground before me. I invoked the powers of the Spirit World, asking them to come to our aid and I prayed it would work.

"It's rising!" Grace's eyes widened in shock, and she took some steps backwards as the luminous spirits from the ground all around us rose up to amass before me. Several of my colleagues were agitated by this.

"Be calm, they are here to help us- hopefully," I said.

Before me, hundreds of luminous figures stood floating just above the ground, all looking at me with distrust in their eyes. I felt every hair in my body tingle, as if a piercing energy ran through it. I slowly found the courage to speak.

"I have summoned you to help us in lighting our way through this void. We need to enter it to find our friend. Will you help us?"

Their wailing was a background noise and for a long minute, no direct response was made. I felt failure wasn't an option, so I stepped closer to the nearest spirits.

"Will not one of you speak with me? I seek your help and the Ivory summons you to our aid." I tried.

A misshapen spirit with markings of torture spoke at last, "Why should we help you? We have suffered enough; we have no wish to enter the Chaos. Nobody would willingly go there. You must be fools." He sneered and others behind him nodded in agreement.

"This is useless!" Grinder hissed behind me. "We'll have to find another way." I glanced behind me and saw several doubtful faces now. I turned back to face the spirits.

"I can see that you have suffered much here and no doubt, are destined to endure an eternity of hardship even in death." I saw several nods and I persevered. "But I can offer you peace if you help us on our quest. A chance never to suffer again. To leave all this terror behind you and never have to endure any more pain in this evil place. How does that sound to you?"

The Spirits were rattled by my words, many grumbling with disbelief. After a few seconds the misshapen spirit spoke again. "How can you possibly promise such a thing? We all know we are destined to suffer here for all eternity, for all the things we have done in our lives. We do not believe you!" They turned to moved away, so I had to act fast.

"Wait!" I called. "This is my proof, and you have my word I will use it."

They turned to see, and their eyes changed in recognition of the Wand of Destruction. All wailing stopped. Silence loomed for a minute, and it was disconcerting to have no sound reverberating in this grim place after the constant background noises.

"You will use it upon us? All of us?" The misshapen man asked warily.

"I promise you I will, as soon as you have finished your task to lead us in and out of that place. I will grant you peace, at last."

The luminous horde nodded finally, and I released the breath I had been holding. I turned to face my colleagues and saw they were smiling. "Come, let's go," I said.

We watched as the luminous green spirits flitted by us, heading straight into the black hole ahead. I prayed that this would work, for it was my only hope of getting through there.

"It's working. They're lighting the way." Hope's eyes lit up with joy.

We followed in the luminescence, watching our feet in case of dangerous drops. There were several. We were surrounded in the green light, which gave us a better view of what was before us. I doubted the Orb could have done better.

"If we'd come in here without a light, we would have all fallen to our doom." Veritas said. I knew he was right and hoped the spirits would remain with us until the end.

Chaos extended outwards dramatically from the initial narrow crack to a vast expanse of gloomy caverns full of rotting carcasses and bones. The smell was dreadful, and I pitied Axl having had to come through here.

"Watch out for the huge gorge to our left." I called, seeing the blackness drop into oblivion.

"We need to cross it to carry on further." The misshapen spirit said.

"Can I ask, what your name was?" I asked the spirit out of curiosity. To my surprise, I saw tears well in his tortured eyes as he sought to remember.

"I was named Darcy long ago," he said. "It was the name my mother gave me, but I haven't heard it used for centuries. You may use it, if you like."

"Well Darcy, it's good to meet you. If you would pause here for a moment while we set ourselves up to cross the gorge, then we can continue on our way." He nodded, unsure what we were about to do. I stepped aside as Stretch moved forward to eye the huge twenty-foot gap.

"Should be no problem." Stretch said. "Just don't go dancing on my back Grinder," he added. With that, he began to elongate his body until it was long enough to bridge the gap, then he gripped the far edge with his hands and dug his feet into the ground on this side.

"Okay, cross quickly." Stretch said, ducking his head down as he formed a bridge with his body. Arch moved away from us and used his leaping powers to leap across the gap instead. He waited on the other side next to Stretch's head to await the others.

We all, one by one, crossed over his body with speed, so as not to put undue strain on him. Once the last one crossed, he retracted his legs over to the far side of the gorge and stood beside us, smiling in triumph.

"I see you have come prepared." Darcy said with an inkling of a first grin on his sorry face.

The expansive cavern spread even wider after the gorge and the light caused by the hundreds of spirits outlined the shape of the caverns, we were in. Spiky fangs protruded from floor and ceiling, some whose points were razor sharp and could easily impale a person should they trip. "Be careful of these points," I said, but all were already wary of them, keeping their distance as they walked.

"What's that?" Grinder exclaimed, as a sudden spurt of steam shot out of the ground ahead of us. Several others began to spit out heat and steam at random points along the way.

"By the gods-" Arch said, shielding us from the closest spout. "They're scalding hot!" He turned to Grinder and said, "Can you do something to make these less of a problem Grinder?"

Grinder stepped closer, nodding, and he waved his hands before him, casting an incantation of reduction onto our surroundings. Very quickly, the steam spouts were reduced in size to mere inches- much safer for us to pass by.

We continued, feeling the heat of lava somewhere beneath our cavern floor, but its golden flow wasn't evident yet. "It seems that this place is riddled with dangers. It's a good job we're all together or we'd be struggling to make it through here." Brava said.

Causia hovered above us within the spirits, keeping an eye out for any hints of the direction we needed to go.

"See anything?" Brava asked her as we treaded carefully.

"Nothing obvi-" Her eyes flashed in alarm as she halted above us. "Oh no. There are Splinters ahead- several of them. Arm yourselves! They've seen us."

My heart lurched as I pictured the hideous creatures, which I'd only seen in picture books in my teachings. They were compiled of lethal shards of needle-sharp slate, which they ejected with extreme force towards any adversary, impaling them to death.

"Arch! Your shield-" I called out urgently. But he was already expanding the shield to accommodate those of us more vulnerable to the splinter ejections. "Patience- you and Hope stay here with Pax and Grace."

Before they got the chance to argue, I had made my way forward with Stretch and the others to attack the Splinters before they got any closer.

Causia was already flying in the heights of the cavern using her powers to crush the Splinters at the front of the group. Beside me, Stretch was emitting fiery beams with his eyes towards others in the pack, causing them to break into smaller pieces, which Brava then hacked to death.

Veritas stood to my left waving his hands towards a group to the left-hand side of the leaders and I grinned as he turned them into stone pillars instead. As Stretch pierced several more, Brava and Grinder- who teleported randomly around the Splinters- hacked them to death.

I ran towards the front to tackle the main horde, whose shards were now flying in the air towards us. I had to duck several times as I invoked the Wand of Destruction's power, and in less than two minutes the Splinters all turned to dust, shards and all.

"Have we got them all?" I called up to Causia.

"Yes, I see no more, they're all dead. We did it!" She smiled down at me and suddenly I heard a strange noise. I looked around to see that the strange sound, almost like the rush of reeds in the breeze, was of our luminous spirits clapping their hands with glee. There was more than one smiling face amongst them now. Darcy looked at us and spoke.

"What are you people? Are you Gods? For I have never seen anyone get the better of any of Veiri Dur's creatures before." I gave a small smile. "No Darcy, we are the Servants of the Wheel, guardians of the Outer World and of Gardia itself. It is our leader that we have come to rescue, with your help."

Darcy's strange face twitched, and his eyes watered visibly. "Then you have our word that we will help you achieve your aim, if you can keep your promise to release us from our misery. You are mighty adversaries, and I am glad to serve you in any way I can." As he finished his words, a chorus of "Aye," was uttered by the spirit horde, all sharing his sentiment.

"We are glad to have you on our side, welcome." Brava said.

Chapter 16

No sooner had we dispatched the Splinters than we met with a new problem as we continued our way into the depths of Chaos. The air here was foul, full of noxious gases and we wrapped anything we could around our noses and mouths as we continued our way through the gloom.

"Gods! What is that?" Hope said as she stepped back in alarm, for out of the very walls around us, clawed arms shot out trying to tear at us with what looked like poison filled talons.

"Keep clear of the walls!" Brava called out, stepping aside to avoid two long arms darting towards her.

Several other lethally taloned arms shot out all around us from the very walls and pillars we passed, and we dodged this way and that to keep from being clawed. We hacked at them where we had no choice but pass, as the cavern divided again into narrower tunnels, which our spirit hosts led us through.

Arch used his Sword of Glass effectively on them. As soon as its blade touched the arms, the whole appendage crumbled to dust. Elsewhere, they were hacked from the walls, to piercing wails as they fell, by our ordinary weapons. Stretch used his beams to cremate the remains.

My eyes saw flashes of moving shadows. I turned my head this way and that, trying to figure what was happening. I felt something else was present in the tunnel, unseen yet.

"Beware- there is something else in here with us, it moves in the shadows unseen, but I sense its presence." I said, my eyes scanning all around me. ."I feel it too." said Hope, her eyes also darting around searching.

We remained still and the arms disappeared. So, they are triggered by motion, I thought to myself. All of us eyed our surroundings whilst remaining still, willing this new menace to show itself.

"Arrgh!" Stretch's voice behind me made my blood turn cold. I turned to see him rapidly turning into an icy statue. I immediately realised then what our adversary was.

"Protect yourselves! It's Shadow- he's in here with us." I called out, my wand at the ready. But in seconds, another Servant fell victim to Shadow's freezing capabilities. To my right, Veritas's elfin face turned into an icy version of himself, his expression that of horror at the realisation of what was happening to him.

"Get behind me!" I yelled to the others, preparing my wand whilst Arch's shield protected the rest from Shadow's grasp. "Show yourself you traitorous vermin." I hissed. "I know it's you Shadow. You're the lowest of the low, betraying your country and your leader like this."

A menacing cackle came from the depths before me before he answered. "You were so slow to find me Mouse and I am not going to make it any easier for you to find me now either. No, you think you're a leader? Huh! That's a joke. You have no idea that I have been following you since the portal, have you? Well, you will get no further. All of you will die right here, right now."

"Aw, come on Shadow- you don't mean that. We've been friends for a long time. What's with you?" Grinder was understandably annoyed. But Shadow did not reply.

I saw it coming before it could hit me. The source point of Shadow's freeze power, a bright dot in the jumble of luminescence. Before it could even advance a few feet towards me, I waved the wand of destruction towards the source and struck.

The blood curdling cry was pitiful. There, before me, Shadow's form transformed just before he died into his normal form, then disintegrated into dust, caught in the Wand's power.

"Mouse, am I? What do you think of me now Shadow?" I said calmly.

An echo of relieved voices and pats on my shoulder told me how the others felt. Only Grinder was quiet, he moved forward to where Shadow's body had crumbled to dust and crouched, touching the ground. He only said one thing, quietly, as though to himself, "Why did I call you my friend?"

"Can you help Stretch and Veritas?" I asked Hope and Pax.

"Yes, of course, I will try." Pax said as Hope nodded.

We waited as Hope firstly touched Stretch's statue of ice. Under her touch, the ice started to thaw, releasing its grip upon its victim. Straight away, Pax laid his own hands on Stretch's body to soothe any pain that the ice had inflicted upon him. In less than two minutes, he appeared back to normal again. Hope hugged him tight with relief. "Thank you, my love," he said before kissing her.

"Thank the gods," Stretch said, his face relaxing again. "I thought for sure that I was going to be cold forever! Thank you, both." They smiled and nodded, moving on to Veritas, to give him the same treatment.

Grace hugged Veritas as soon as he was released from the ice's grip and Pax's final touch had him feeling well again. He kissed her gently on her lips and hugged her tight, smiling at every one in relief. "Not a pleasant feeling being an ice statue," Veritas said. "I don't recommend it."

"And to think he has been working alongside us for centuries as one of the team." Stretch said with a shudder.

"I guess you never really know people if they've got something to hide."

"I was so wrong- I really thought he was my friend." Grinder's voice was barely audible, and his face was pale. His eyes held the weight of the world within them. Brava stepped forward and spoke to him. "Don't feel so bad Grinder- he fooled us all- perhaps even Axl herself."

"Yes," I said. "None of us could have known of this side to him. I wonder what Pinni promised him?"

Several looked up at me. "You think he sought to rule with Pinni?" Grace asked.

"Quite possibly. But I wouldn't trust Pinni to keep any of his promises. I think as soon as he'd got what he wanted, he would discard Shadow like dirty laundry." That got a few smiles at least.

"Well, we should keep going," said Brava. "I think we might be getting close if Shadow was here. Are we ready?" She held up her sword and shield as she eyed us all up.

"Aye, let's go." Veritas replied, standing alongside Grace. More claws inevitably shot out, but we were prepared now and each was tackled without mercy and soon we were emerging into a different section.

"Now what?" Grace asked, looking from one ancient door to another.

We stood in an almost circular segment, with three iron doors encased in cobwebs at eight-foot intervals in the cave wall before us. There was no inkling of what was beyond the doors, so I looked to Darcy.

"Do you know which doorway we need to go through?" I asked.

"Actually no- this is as far as any of us have been. I think there's an enchantment on the doors preventing us from crossing through them." He went to the door ahead and tried to disappear through it to prove his point and we saw his spirit ejected backwards by a mere touch of the door.

"Okay, now what do we do?" Grinder asked. "I could try teleporting beyond the door, but if there's no spirit light to guide me beyond, I would probably see nothing anyway."

"In any case, it might be dangerous for you to try and cross the doors if they're enchanted." Brava replied.

We stood thinking about a plan. "We need to break the enchantment on the doors somehow." Stretch said, reading my thoughts. I nodded, thinking hard.

"I have an idea," I said.

Whilst the others watched my back, I stood before the three doors as I invoked the Stone of Power's ability to destroy things. I hoped it would destroy the charms set on the doors.

The stone did something that it hadn't done before when I invoked its power. The stone trembled softly in my palm at first, giving off a few puffs of the noxious gas that we had encountered. Then, as I concentrated more on the stone's powers, the trembling turned into a violent shaking, and I was forced to enclose the artefact between both my cupped hands to stop it flying off. It now spewed out a dense cloud of gas and everyone tightened their protective masks urgently to prevent suffocation. Stretch's elongated arm held my scarf tightly in place on my own face, for which I was grateful.

A loud cracking noise filled the space but because of the gas, I could not see what was breaking. I became vaguely aware of Veritas' voice chanting something behind me and seconds later, the gas had disappeared, replaced by droplets of water. Now I could see what the noise had been.

The stone stilled in my hands and the doors before me each bore a deep diagonal crack from top to bottom, and I could sense the enchantment had lifted. I turned to thank Veritas for the transfiguration and the water droplets ceased as soon as they began. The stone had done its job.

"Can you enter the doors now?" I asked Darcy. "The charm has been lifted. We need to know what is beyond each door." Darcy nodded and floated towards the doors with four of his fellow spirits following. Pax stepped forward to go through the solid doors, but I stopped him.

"No Pax, wait until they come back. There might still be dangers for us beyond those doors."

Darcy and some fellow spirits took the left-hand door, while two other groups entered through the other doors. We waited and waited.

"What's taking them so long?" Grinder asked, his patience waning.

"It might be a while until they get to-" I was abruptly brought to a halt when the group that went through the centre door re-emerged. An elderly spirit spoke for the group.

"We don't think you'll find your leader through this door, beyond are the fires of Veiri Dur, an evil place. It is filled with burning pits where the dead suffer torment before entering the spirit world. It is a place of misery and pain. More than one of us have been tortured this way in the past."

"You saw no sign of her from the description we gave you? Are you sure?" Brava asked, frustration building in her as she paced before us.

Before they could answer, Darcy's group emerged from the left-hand door. He shook his head.

"Your friend isn't there, or if she was, she no longer lives." Darcy said sombrely.

"What do you mean? What did you see?" Arch asked. Stretch almost vomited to the side and I imagined he had read Darcy's mind.

"You really want to know?" Darcy asked softly. Despite Stretch's shake of the head, the others nodded.

In there are the tortured souls after Veiri Dur has finished with them. Their bodies burnt and sliced, brutally beaten to death before being incarcerated in tar pits. It's truly horrible." All of us were stunned and tears fell freely from our eyes. I prayed to the gods that Axl hadn't suffered the same fate.

We waited for the final group to return from the right-hand door, hoping that they had better news for us. It was a slim hope, but better than the alternative. After ten more minutes they returned.

"We found your leader." One of the returning spirits said.

Pax moved forward through the door with some of our spirits as we prepared to break it open further with Stretch's eye beams. We stood back as he cut through the iron door to create an opening wide enough for us all to walk through. With the last sizzle of the powerful beam, the heavy door groaned then tilted backwards to crash onto the floor behind.

Pax was stood twenty feet away inside the tunnel with the spirits, as we entered. It looked like most of the ordinary tunnels we expected to find in an underground lair at first. But Pax pointed to the floor, for us to be careful, for there again, were random pits accessing chasms below the path.

"Watch your feet everyone." I called, as the spirits led the way. And very soon we came to a wide lava filled chasm which blocked our path forward. It was too dangerous for Stretch to bridge it with his body this time.

"I'll deal with it," said Hope, stepping to the front, her green hair at odds with the bright orange of the lava.

"Be careful my love." Stretch said to her and she nodded with a smile.

We waited as she commanded control of the elements before us. Her hand whipped up an ice storm, focused on the chasm alone and as the freezing wind pierced the lava field it began to dim and cool before our eyes, hissing as the steam spat out, as it solidified. She kept the ice storm going until satisfied that the lava was no longer a danger to us. She prodded the crust with her sword, and it gave a metallic sound that echoed across the tunnel.

"It's safe to cross now. We can walk on it," she said. She led the way, with Stretch and Pax by her side, in case her powers were needed again.

The tunnel got wider and wider as we walked over to the other side, the pits lessening until finally there were no more. Instead, we found ourselves surrounded by sounds of murmuring creatures in the shadows. Bats?

"Look out!" Pax called as he swung his sword through the disturbed throng descending from ledges and shadows all around us. "Vampire bats!"

We fought with everything in our possession to prevent being bitten by these creatures, Arch shielding several of us with the Shield of Darkness as we scythed our swords through them. Those with bows found it impossible to strike so many and left it to Stretch, Causia and those of us with powers to defend us from their bites.

Causia destroyed hundreds that came close to the shield with her powers and Hope and Stretch burnt several more with their abilities. I used the wand of Destruction on any that survived to good effect. From the edge of the Shield, Veritas conjured up a transfiguration spell that caught hundreds more in its grasp, turning them to falling leaves instead. With our combined effort, we survived the attack relatively unscathed.

"Couldn't you have warned us about all these things in our way?" Grinder looked at the spirits angrily. Darcy merely shrugged and said, "Obviously, they didn't sense our presence, being spirits, and in any case, you should be prepared for anything knowing where you are."

Grinder looked at him and sniffed loudly then gave a harumph before walking away, striking the walls with his sword for good measure.

Hope dropped to the floor gasping. In seconds, Stretch was at her side, holding her shoulders in his arms. "What is it my love? Were you bitten?" She was unconscious already, her head drooping to his knee. Pax rushed to their aid, scouring Hope's limbs for signs of a bite.

"She's been bitten- twice on her back." Pax said, pulling out his knife. Patience instantly dropped onto her knees to aid him. "Place her on her side, Stretch- quickly!" Pax said. He nodded to Patience as he prepared to gouge out the poison from the wounds with his dagger. Patience laid her hands on Hope's body and soon her skin glowed from her soothing touch, taking away all her pain. Pax dug out the black venom with the point of his dagger, flicking the poison onto the ground, then again with the second wound. Hope did not flinch, for Patience took away all her pain.

Pax daubed the wounds with a clean cloth soaked in alcohol from the Horn of Plenty and soon her black wound began to turn pink. Finally, Pax rested his healing hands upon Hope's skin, and we observed the rapid regeneration of flesh, healthy and clean once more. Her eyes shot open, and she took a breath. Stretch was holding her hand and now he scooped her up in his arms and embraced her tightly, tears running down his cheek.

"Thank you- both of you." Stretch said, looking up at Patience and Pax.

"Yes, thank you," Hope added, "for I'm assuming you healed me from a vampire bite?"

"Two actually." Stretch said with a small smile. He helped her up and in moments we were mobile again.

The expanse before us was vast, lit by lava oozing out of the walls on two sides, pooling into a long channel that led across the cavern. A huge creature fought with another, fifty paces away in a rocky basin, as several misshapen demons and orcs gathered to watch the fight. Some joined in the fight, throwing spears or knives at one or another of the combatants, causing others to gang up to fight each other in the periphery.

We watched from the shadow of Arch's shield, looking for signs of our leader. A sudden horrendous howl shook our bones, as one of the combatants had a piece of his stomach hacked away in the fight, spilling his intestines to the floor. The victor screeched with triumph as several minions pushed the dying creature into the lava channel to be engulfed to its death more swiftly.

Another fight spilled over among the minions and more fell or were pushed to their deaths into the lava to join the victim. "Look!" Brava pointed to a steam filled area beyond the lava pit, where a rock shelf was elevated above the battle basin. A dark figure in a cloak stood watching the fight and looked to be ordering another creature to do something. Pinni.

Chapter 17

The spirits waited out of sight, back beyond the bend in the tunnel, now that we could see from the lava's glow what was before us. We didn't want their presence to warn Pinni we were here.

"We must be careful not to fall into one of Pinni's enchantments." Stretch spoke into our minds so as not to cause unnecessary sound. We nodded; sure Pinni would have good hearing despite his age. We all had to try and think of the best plan to get to him before he got to us. We didn't want to make it so far, only to succumb to his powers at the last minute.

"Do you think we will be shielded even from him by the Shield of Darkness?" Stretch asked. I nodded, for I knew the Shield had been taken from Veiri Dur himself in the

Battle of Noor centuries earlier. Anything that belonged to him would have such powers as to fool Pinni.

Brava waved her hand towards the easiest route for us across the cavern, avoiding the lava streams and Veiri Dur's creatures. We all nodded, seeing the faint outline of a gradient in the rocks where we could ascend to reach Pinni on his higher ledge. If we got that far under cover of the shield, we could then overcome him in surprise.

It was risky, we knew that. We had no idea if we would be discovered by some creature's exceptional sense of smell or hearing, but it was our only way of getting there.

We all knew that we were a little too far away for Veritas to use transfiguration on any of the creatures yet, but if we got closer-

We moved swiftly, our weapons at the ready, the Shield covering us from sight. The heat from the lava pools was intense as we neared the channels and Brava led us carefully across her chosen path of least resistance. Around the bend in the channel we passed, sweat dripping from our bodies. This was the point closest to the Daemons on the basin.

My senses were on high alert, and I immediately saw a large, truncated creature turn his snout and sniff the air towards us. "He can smell our sweat!" Stretch's voice entered our minds as one. He took a few steps closer to us and we hurried away from the intense heat source and began the incline up to Pinni's platform. I watched the creature as we went.

The creature moved around still sniffing the air and Pinni noticed it. "What is it Gufflong, what troubles you?" Pinni's acrid voice asks.

"I smell man flesh and sweat Leader." The creature replied. Pinni's eyes darted around in panic and his hands raised up to cast a spell.

"Oh no- he's casting a reveal spell!" Stretch said.

"Keep going," my mind sent back, "we will not be revealed under the Shield." Arch hesitated for a second and Hope almost stepped out of the Shield's embrace, where she would be revealed, but Stretch pulled her back just in time and urged Arch to be more careful.

We saw Pinni's frustration as nothing was revealed by his spell and we were now closing in on his level. His head spun around, looking for what was around him. I knew he suspected our presence.

Brava couldn't help it. She gasped in horror at the sight beyond Pinni and Pinni's gaze locked on our position.

We saw the terrible sight together, there, beyond Pinni at the back of the stone platform. She clung onto life despite the odds, her body ravaged by torture. Tied upright onto a slab of rock, Axl, bloodied and with arms hacked off, her head hung in pain, had only her incredible remnants of determination to keep her alive. I wept at the sight myself and none of us could contain our anger any longer.

Some ran towards Axl's aid and others charged towards Pinni to bring him down. Arch and Brava led the charge and I followed with my heart full of hatred and disgust at what Pinni had done.

Pinni's eyes shot up in alarm at seeing so many of us here together. He flailed, calling out to his demons to attack before we reached him. But Veritas was already at the front of the dais with Grinder, dealing with the creatures. One reducing the size of the foul creatures whilst the other began to transfigure them into mice. They scattered around, confused.

As Pinni realised he was surrounded and without aid, he did something I had never seen before- an ancient magic, which I had once heard of, but did not quite believe.

As we rushed up to him, he enveloped himself in a darkness so absolute that nothing could be seen in it. But still we charged, slicing forward with our weapons. Brava shouted, "Stop hiding you coward, show yourself! Fight like a man. You deserve this you venomous Durin!"

But the darkness dissipated instantly to reveal Pinni had disappeared, like he had teleported himself. We were cutting through the air impotently.

"Where's he gone?" Arch's voice was full of hatred. I hadn't heard him speak so forcefully before.

"It looks like he's teleported somewhere- keep your eyes on the lookout for him re-appearing somewhere else." Brava called, her own eyes shifting uneasily about.

"You won't find him." I said and they glanced at me strangely for a second.

"Why not Blender?" Stretch asked.

"The magic he used, it's an ancient one. He has not simply teleported himself, he has left our world entirely, gone to another dimension. A place where he cannot be found." They stared- at first doubting me, but only briefly.

"He's gone?" Brava asked simply. I nodded.

"He will not return, not for a long while. I read that this magic can only be used once in a cycle of Sol." They looked at me in shock.

"So, the bastard has escaped punishment- for now!" Arch spoke harshly again. I nodded.

"We need help over here!" Patience called from the back of the rock platform, where she tended Axl with Pax and Causia. They had lain her on the floor, destroying her chains. Her whole body was blanched with loss of blood.

We ran over and focused our attention on our beloved Guardian. She was unrecognisable. Her face, pale and blood streaked, swollen from beatings and her arms gone. The stumps raw and oozing.

"I need to heal her and Causia can regenerate her limbs," Pax said. "But she is so weak, it might kill her, and I don't know how to give her enough strength to survive this."

I knew what to do instinctively. I don't know how, but as Axl's faded eyes caught mine, the thought sprang into my mind instantly. She closed her eyes then and a faint smile touched her lips.

"I know how we can give her strength to survive this." I spoke clearly so all could hear in their panic. They silenced and looked to me in anticipation. They believed in me; I could see it in their eyes, and no one challenged me. "What do we do?" Hope asked, her face calm and accepting.

So, we formed a human chain, linking arms tightly, ready to concentrate all our energies upon Axl. Pax began the chain to one side of Axl, his free hand ready to touch Axl's stump to heal her body. At the other end of the chain was Patience then Causia, ready to soothe her pain and regenerate her limbs. Touching her other stump.

We are ready for you Blender." Hope said, her eyes watching me intently as they all circled around Axl and myself. I nodded. I hoped I was right in what I had to do and my whole being felt it was what Axl needed. So, without further preamble, I laid myself gently upon Axl's body, head-to-head, torso to torso, legs to legs and closed my eyes as my body blended into hers.

Many of the Servants hadn't seen me do a blending before and there were a few gasps as I disappeared into Axl's body. My arms stretched out to touch each end of the circle, upon Causia and Pax's hands, making a complete circuit.

"I'm ready, tell everyone to start now." I said to Stretch telepathically. "He's ready," said Stretch, "we can all start our concentration now."

The circuit of Servants began to glow with power as each added their energy to Axl's ravaged body. Their eyes closed in concentration, I saw the circuit intensify with light, almost filling this entire cavern with its glow.

I felt Axl's body stir as their energies and strength began to return into her bloodstream and within minutes, I knew she was ready to receive Causia and Pax's ministrations.

"You may begin to regenerate her limbs now." Stretch said to Pax and Causia as he read my thoughts.

The power that ran through into her body intensified as the two began their tasks and I could sense a background sensation of Axl's pain being relieved by Patience's connection in the circuit.

The circuit worked as one- relieving, regenerating, and healing her ravaged body, the heat intensifying inside her as the healing began. Slowly, I felt movement run below my arms, as Causia's skill caused Axl's own arms to regenerate. The movement ran slowly from shoulder to fingertip, with blood returning to fill her veins and restore sensation. I was the catalyst in the restoration, and I was glad of my powers right then. Without me being a part of Axl, there might not have been the possibility of full restoration,

Axl gasped, drawing in a healthy new breath, the strongest in a long time. Her voice entered my head. "Thank you, Blender, I knew I had chosen well when I sent you on your quest, both for Brava and ultimately, for myself. Without you, it would have failed."

I gasped with surprise. She knew. She knew she was going to be abducted like this...

I released myself from the blending and Stretch told the circuit the restoration was complete. They opened their eyes just as I stepped up before them again.

Never had I seen so much joy in people's faces as I did then. Even Grinder was smiling broadly, as Axl stood before us now, fully restored, and healthy again. Her smile filled our hearts and souls once more.

"Thank you all for what you have done. You realised that working together, you can defeat anyone or anything. I am very proud of you all, but especially of you Blender, you have proven to be the wisest and most courageous of all of us, to have ventured to such dark places and confront the darkest horrors on your way here.

"Hear hear!" The others chorused and clapped as one. I had never felt so embarrassed as then, but I managed to embrace the sentiment, for it was earnest, I knew.

"How did you make your way down into these dark bowels of misery?" Axl asked, seeing our weapons. "I know the Orb of Light would not work down here."

I turned to face the tunnel from the direction we came. "Darcy! You can all come forth now." I called.

Axl's face was a picture of admiration and surprise at seeing all the luminous spirits rush forth from the tunnels to join us. They surrounded us, eyeing the confused mice darting about the floor.

"You continue to amaze me Blender- for I assume this was your idea?" I nodded as she glanced my way. "I had not thought of you using the spirits to guide you. Well played!"

I mentioned the deal I had made with Darcy and the other tortured spirits and she agreed it was a good bargain. So, they carefully led us back, out of this loathsome maze in the rocks, through the dangerous tunnels and caverns once more, as we updated Axl on what had been happening since her betrayal. She knew some of it herself, somehow- her powerful magic playing a part there.

"It was a brilliant idea to clone all of you Hope," she said, "and I am so relieved to hear that the Window on the World has been saved. Thank you, Grinder and Pax."

"We knew it was vital for when we retrieved you Great Leader," said Grinder. I marvelled at this different side to him, how circumstances can change a person so dramatically. Shadow was beyond saving, his heart and soul turned black by Veiri Dur, but Grinder, well, he showed his worth several times over.

We emerged out of the absolute darkness of Chaos at last, guided safely, as promised by Darcy and the others, to the Bone plateau. I turned to the spirits and addressed them all. "Thank you all, dear spirits. You have redeemed yourselves for past sins by your actions today and I will keep my promise to you all." I held out my Wand of Destruction and bowed deeply with the other Servants before invoking the power of the wand, to give the spirits eternal peace.

As the luminosity faded, a heavy weight lifted from the air around us and the very bones beneath our feet dissolved into nothing. They were gone and the weight of their torture gone with them and the last sight that stuck with me was the relief and joy on all their faces as they left this world.

Chapter 18

The way back was different. Axl wanted to make sure Veiri Dur was out of Gardia, so she summoned the Winged horses as we made our way through the Veil.

"Where is he revealed through the Window on the World?" Axl asked Stretch as we waited for the horses to arrive. Stretch communicated telepathically with his clone in Gardia to find out.

"He's at the Great Divide, amassing an army of Demons as we speak." Stretch said. "Good, close enough to where I want him to be. Come, let's be on our way, the horses are here." Axl said.

I didn't see anything in the sky from the plateau where we stood, just grey skies full of bad weather. But seconds later, they appeared before us, landing elegantly, a horse stopping in front of each of us as if made to order.

"Hello Beauty," said Patience to her horse. "I hope we didn't wake you up from a pleasant dream." Brava looked at her oddly as she placed her hand on Spirit's reins.

"Do horses dream? Really?" She asked, deftly leaping onto her charge with one swift movement. Sprit raised his head and whinnied in greeting. "Of course, they do- all animals do." Patience replied with a tap onto her horse's muzzle.

I mounted Lightning, hoping he still remembered me and clung onto the reins in case he lifted off without warning. He did. We all soared into the air as one, a small cloud of living beings, powerful and purposeful. The horses seemed to know where to go. Maybe Axl had told them using her mind, like Stretch maybe? I didn't ask.

Axl's own steed was superb, blue black, glistening with health, its ebony mane highlighted by silver in this light. It was bright eyed and eager to be on its way, leading the company forward, like a soldier leading the charge.

I wondered what its name was, but of course, Stretch read my mind and responded immediately. "His name is Jet and he's the fastest of the winged horses, I'm told." I smiled back and nodded across at my friend, who rode to my left.

We flew over a vast expanse of Gardia, over snow filled fields and valleys, high snowy crags and through sleet filled clouds over the plains to the south, where the highest mountains loomed in the distance.

"What's that?" Grace asked as she spotted the smoke of several fires in the distance, dotted far apart. They weren't ordinary campfires; they were villages burning.

"Oh no.." Brava's keen eyes spotted scores of dead villagers strewn across the land around the fires. "He's attacked the villages and killed the inhabitants."

"Look- some survivors are running away towards the forests below us." Hope pointed. "Do you think they will be safe there?"

Axl replied, "They will be now." She waved her new limbs into a circle; its form sparkling with energy and hurled it down to the forest below. It created a barrier that would protect the villagers from harm. She urged Jet on, and they quickly distanced themselves from the rest of us.

"Where's she going?" Grace asked, eyeing her mount veering to the right. "Oh- Guerremots- a swarm of them." Grace looked over at us, wondering if we should follow Axl to attack the winged monsters. But the answer came quickly.

From Axl's fingers, jets of white-hot fire shot out towards the muscular Guerremots, incinerating their wings with its touch. Each creature, half man, half bat, dropped to its death upon contact with Axl's fire. They tried to fire lethal arrows at her before they succumbed to the heat, but Axl had already invoked a shield around herself, and they merely bounced right back.

"She's amazing isn't she." Hope watched her easily defeat the swarm without batting an eyelid and we all could only marvel at her powers. It was no wonder that she had been leader of Gardia all this time.

"Look- there are other swarms further to the South, circling that dark area. What is that do you think?" Hope pointed towards the strange shape.

"It's Veiri Dur- he's opening up Chaos, by-passing the Veil." Brava said, her nostrils flaring with anger. She urged Spirit on to join Axl ahead and we all followed with great urgency.

The dark shape was growing visibly, with demon hordes swarming out of its bowels, all manner of foul beings spewed out of the chasm that cleaved the ground ahead.

"Rock giants and Mud trolls- I thought they were a myth," Arch said, as we saw them thumping out of the darkness to join the orcs and other misanthropic creatures. The ground boiled with their movement, turning the pristine snow black with poisonous intent.

We looked to each other; our faces locked in worry. "How can we hope to fight all these creatures?" Grace asked, her face pale.

Axl heard and her head turned toward us, and she smiled confidently, "Small change." She said and flew directly towards the heart of the infestation.

In shock, we followed, weapons drawn in readiness for whatever was to come our way. Already, Causia was casting her destruction web below her, and hundreds of demons crumbled to dust into the snow. And Stretch emitted his powerful beams with his eyes, cremating the closest of Veiri Dur's creatures.

Below us, the horde began to notice our presence and a painfully piercing roar tore towards us from the heart of the blackness. Veiri Dur. Axl sped towards the spot where he raged against our presence without hesitation, cutting a swathe through the horde ranks below her with her powerful magic. They fell to the ground like scythed wheat, never to rise again.

I waved my wand of destruction towards the evil beings as they came close enough, and I had to dodge various missiles as they came flying through the air towards me. But Lightning was quicker than their aim and she kept me out of danger as I cast my wand.

"What the?" Pax laughed and I looked towards where he stared. Below him were pigs and geese squeaking and squawking their way along the ground. I glanced towards Veritas, and he was smiling broadly at his handiwork.

"Good job." I waved with a grin, and he nodded before letting loose more transfiguration spells upon the unsuspecting horde.

It was then that he entered my mind. I almost dropped my wand in surprise as images of evil filled my head, my friends spiked onto poles, their blood cascading out of their bodies onto the tarnished snow below.

"No!" I yelled, holding my head to blot them out, but they persisted, bringing with them agonising pain.

"What is it Blender?" Patience pulled alongside me; her face contorted with worry.

"It's Veiri Dur- He's invading my mind with images of our destruction." I replied, the pain that accompanied the images was terrible- as though a thousand spears were piercing my body all at once.

She did not hesitate. She leapt onto Lightning beside me and placed her hands on my head. Their warmth imbued me with a sense of peace and calm and very quickly I was in another place entirely, a peaceful place, full of wildflowers and babbling brooks- my favourite place in Gardia.

I became aware of her voice now, calming and soothing the pain away. The images were gone, replaced by thoughts of friendship and camaraderie of the weeks past, as we fought together to restore peace to our land.

I opened my eyes finally, feeling better than I had done in a long time. Patience's eyes bore into mine, searching for something. "Has the pain gone?" she asked, and I nodded.

"Thank you, Patience. I needed that," I said.

With a smile, she leapt back onto her own horse, which was waiting patiently for her to return, and we both re-joined the battle.

What was happening? We both found ourselves staring at a different scene below us. There were no demons moving, in fact, all of Dur's creatures lay incinerated or inert on the ground below us. The crack had stilled, but at its centre a terrible battle was about to begin.

213

At the heart of the darkness, a glowing ember moved, expanding as it approached the horrified form of Veiri Dur. I saw Jet, riderless, standing amongst the corpses at the edge of the darkness, its rider intent on justice.

"Gods! She's going to tackle him alone!" Patience said as we descended to re-join the others. They were hovering a hundred feet above the chasm.

"Why aren't you going to help her?" I asked, looking to my colleagues desperately.

"We can't," said Veritas. "She has cast a warding spell on us. We can't get any closer. I guess she wants us to be safe. We all know how powerful Veiri Dur is." His face was grim for once, frustrated at our impotence.

"Exactly-" I said. "That's why we need to help her. We can't let her confront him alone. Can't we counter her spell?" "No," Brava's voice was curt. She looked at me. "You forget, Axl's the only one who can counter Veiri Dur. It's because of her power that he has been kept in the realms of Chaos for all these centuries past."

"But he got out, Pinni helped him." Grinder said, for once, he was backing me up and it felt odd.

"He only got out because Pinni cut off Axl's source of power- her arms." Brava replied. "He knew exactly what he had to do to allow Veiri Dur to enter the Outer World. But now that Axl's arms are restored, her power is also restored. You should have more faith in her."

I felt ashamed. I knew she was right. We all knew Axl
was the reason Gardia and the Outer World had been safe
for thousands of years from the forces of evil. It was only
through treachery and deceit that her power was
temporarily taken away from her.

I looked down at the scene with the others, willing our
Leader to prevail. Axl was easy to find in the darkness,
with her circle of power aflame around her as she moved
towards Veiri Dur. Now he too, surrounded himself with a
barrier of some sort- perhaps a shield to ward off Axl's
power? Its violet glow vibrated as he moved further back
into the shadows.

A sudden lance of energy hurtled out of the violet ring
towards Axl, but she didn't even flinch. She swatted the
lance aside as though it was a meddlesome fly and it
dispersed to the floor. She pressed forward as he tried
again, with equal results. Now he tried casting spells
upon her, but they all bounced off her ember field
impotently.

"He's afraid." Hope said. "He knows he can't win."

"He's thinking of running." Stretch said with a grin and at
that moment, he began to run. But Axl hurled forth a
Spike-Snatch, and it latched onto Veiri Dur's body,
pulling him closer to Axl.

He struggled in its grip, but the more he moved, the
deeper the spikes entered his flesh. He cried out in pain as
Axl pulled him towards her. He struggled to free one
hand and in seconds, unleashed a fiery lance at Axl. But
again, it bounced off her ember circle impotently.

She held him in the Spike-Snatch ten feet from where she stood, and the spiky web lifted him off the ground as Axl raised her right hand. We watched as Veiri Dur's captured body spun at an ever-increasing speed in the air around Axl. His screams intensified as the speed increased into a volatile tornado that lifted debris lying around into its vortex.

All the detritus of the demon corpses and ashes were sucked up into the vortex until the ground was cleared of all the creatures' remains. As soon as the last trace of evidence had been sucked into this now much engorged tornado, Axl hurled the vortex deep into the heart of the chasm. The sound of Veiri Dur's screams faded as he was ejected back into his own domain.

Axl stepped back from the edge of the chasm and raised her arms. I could see she was chanting something in a strange language and with it, her arms glowed like gold. Shards of gold speared out of her limbs, spreading wide over the darkened ground as she twirled full circle.

"Oh look!" Grace was spellbound, as were many of us, for we had not seen such power before. Everywhere the gold touched, the ground transformed back to its former colour. The snow was pristine once more and the chasm was gone entirely, leaving no trace of its presence.

We gasped in admiration and suddenly our horses began to descend towards Axl. She had lifted the warding.

Her face was radiant, her eyes betrayed no sign of her ill treatment, bar a streak of blood across her face. Causia swept her hand before Axl, restoring her clothing to its former grandeur and casting aside any trace of blood. Axl smiled.

"Thank you Causia. Indeed, thank you all for getting us to this point. You have saved our land, and all of Gardia and the Outer Worlds owe you, their gratitude. I am truly proud of you- each and every one of you."

This was praise indeed, but we hadn't done it for the praise, we did it because it was right.

"Is Veiri Dur dead?" Grace asked.

"No, he does not get away so easily. He's back where he belongs, with all his other foul creatures, to suffer an eternity of misery in Chaos." Axl said.

"But what if he gets out again?" Grace asked. Axl smiled. "He won't, he can't, now that I am back in power again the chasm will not open, not for him, nor for Pinni."

"But when Pinni returns, will he not side with Veiri Dur again?" Arch asked.

Axl looked calm and relaxed. "Pinni can't get back for a year yet and when he does, we'll be ready for him. Now, who's ready to restore some villages and their inhabitants?"

We all smiled and re-mounted our horses, ready to return to our day jobs. Pinni can wait for another day.

The End

Story continues in Book 2 of the Servants of the Wheel.

AUTHOR BIOGRAPHY

Beth Schluter was born in Wales and grew up in Bala, North Wales, in the picturesque Snowdonia National Park. After becoming a Specialist Teacher of Languages, Music and Art in a Late Primary School in Northwest London, Beth took early retirement after 30 years of teaching. She wanted to pursue her dream of becoming a novelist, and a year after retiring, Beth was signed up by international publishers, William & Brown and Argus Better Books.

For six consecutive years, they published her Science-Fiction novels, The Earth Fleet series. In 2021, Beth started to self-publish her Fantasy series, Servants of the Wheel, with Amazon, finding great joy in writing.

Beth's other interests are gardening, knitting and Art. Beth is secretary to her local Art Club and continues to paint in oils, acrylics and pastels and has sold many artworks over the years. She now lives in rural Essex, in the little village of Galleywood, not far from Chelmsford.

ACKNOWLEDGEMENTS

Thank you to Bill O'Connor for allowing my dream to come true and believing in me. Thank you also for the ease of publishing at Amazon.

Other Books in the series:

Book 2- Black Mass

Book 3- The Cursed

Printed in Great Britain
by Amazon

33561831R00128